Submission

Marthe Blau

Submission

Translated from the French by Howard Curtis

ATRIA BOOKS
New York London Toronto Sydney

ATRIA BOOKS
1230 Avenue of the Americas
New York, NY 10020

Copyright © 2003 by Éditions Jean-Claude Lattès
Translation copyright © 2005 by Howard Curtis

Originally published in France in 2003 as *Entre Ses mains* by Éditions Jean-Claude Lattès.

This translation first published in Great Britain in 2005 by Transworld Publishers, A Division of The Random House Group Ltd.

Published by arrangement with Transworld Publishers, A Division of The Random House Group Ltd.

For information address Atria Books, 1230 Avenue of the Americas, New York, NY 10020.

Library of Congress Cataloging-in Publication Data

Blau, Marthe.
[Entre ses mains. English]
Submission : a novel / Marthe Blau ; translated from the French by Howard Curtis.
    p. cm.
 I. Curtis, Howard, date. II. Title.

PQ2702.L38E6713 2005
843'.92—dc22   2004062764

ISBN-13: 978-0-7432-7104-2
ISBN-10:   0-7432-7104-1

First Atria Books hardcover edition July 2005

10 9 8 7 6 5 4 3 2 1

ATRIA BOOKS is a trademark of Simon & Schuster, Inc.

Manufactured in the United States of America

For information about special discounts for bulk purchases, please contact Simon & Schuster Special Sales at 1-800-456-6798 or business@simonandschuster.com.

For B.V.

"We must dare to be what we are, hold fast to it and, if need be, we must learn when to give way to the new gods. We must know how to die."

—GABRIEL MATZNEFF

Submission

I

I'm in front of the porte cochere and my life is passing before me. There's a knot in my stomach and my legs sway on my heels. I can't go on.

All of a sudden, I feel very cold, or very hot, I'm not sure which. I think about my baby, my darling boy, my reason for living. I see again the look in his eyes when I left him in the arms of a babysitter he doesn't know very well.

Where am I? What am I doing here, shaved and scented, teetering on black stilettos with pointed toes and three-and-a-half-inch heels, and wearing an uncomfortable garter belt and a G-string that cuts into my skin?

My stomach hurts. I think of leaving, running back to my wonderful son and hugging him and telling him how much I love him, how I'll never leave him, how I'll dedicate my life to him.

I see again the day he was born, the tears of joy when he came out, the emotion on his daddy's face, the vows we made, the loving kisses, the osmosis that binds the three of us.

And I punch in the entry code for the building.

He's here in front of me. He was waiting for me. He doesn't say hello, just kisses me on my right cheek and puts an arm around my shoulders and pulls me inside.

I'm shaking under my leather coat. I try to control it but can't. I can't speak either. All I can do is smile weakly. What's about to happen is going to change my life. I don't want to cheat on my husband, but I already know that in a little while, when I leave here, when I leave Him, I'll be a different person. I remember the night of my eighteenth birthday, my first boyfriend trying to explain what love is.

He doesn't say a word.

He just looks at me, keeps looking at me, staring at me.

His eyes are gray. I know He's unstoppable. But the last thing I want is for Him to stop.

Very slowly, He unbuttons my coat. The leather squeaks beneath His fingers.

I haven't moved an inch. The coat falling to the floor makes me jump.

He takes my hands in His, and for the first time our skins touch. He squeezes my fingers and I go dizzy with excitement.

I'd like to kiss Him. I don't dare.
    I'd like Him to kiss me. He doesn't.
    He just looks at me.
    He still hasn't said a word.

Slowly, He squeezes my hands and pushes me toward the sofa.
    Once on the sofa, I sit up very straight, with my knees together.
    His eyes move over my body. I lower my head. The small of my back feels stiff because of the way I'm sitting.

My mouth is dry.
    I see a bottle of water on the coffee table and reach out my hand.
    He stops me.
    "No."
    It's the first word He's uttered, and His voice carries me away.
    I forget my thirst.

◆ ◆ ◆

No sound comes from my throat. I can't take my eyes off His hands—or my mind. My body is already waiting for their touch. I say nothing. I savor the waiting, the waiting for Him.

His gray eyes again.

He reaches out His hand to the back of my neck.

I think He's going to take me in His arms, but He doesn't.

His forefinger touches my skin, moves down my throat and lightly over my breast through the silk that's covering it and along the curve of my hip, down to my legs. With infinite slowness, He lifts the material and uncovers my black stockings, my white thighs.

My heart is pounding. I suck in air, hardly able to breathe. I lower my eyes.

I listen to the silence.

A heavy, penetrating, all-pervasive silence, like the silence of a desert abandoned by every living thing. I'm a carcass of flesh at the mercy of a mad demon who's going to take me away on his red horse.

I watch Him as he lifts my dress above my stockings, as if I were no longer me. I no longer feel as if I'm me. I've lost possession of my strength, my willpower, my consciousness. I'm no longer me.

I'm still sitting with my knees together.

I hear His breathing, faster now as the sight of my white skin excites Him.

I'm afraid, and tortured with desire.

Nobody has ever looked at me like Him.

He's lifted the front of my dress as far as my hips.

He lets go of the material and takes a step back. I feel His eyes on me, focused between my legs, like an incision.

I savor those burning eyes on me, penetrating me.

I want Him. I'm His. From now on, I'm His and nobody else's.

I want Him to kiss me but He doesn't.

My body screams soundlessly for His hands but He doesn't touch me.

"Open."

I jump.

"Open your legs." His voice has gotten harder.

My knees are still stuck together.

◆ ◆ ◆

"Obey now. Open your legs."

Nobody has ever spoken to me like Him.

This time, my knees knock together and I can't stop the shaking.

"Open them! Open them or leave! I want to see you."

The threat of being thrown out is like a jolt to my brain, and finally I obey.

He stares at me for a while, then at last walks up to me and reaches out his hand to touch the black material over my swelling cunt.

He strokes the fabric with precise fingers.

I hear my heart.

I hear His breathing.

He's knelt in front of the sofa, between my spread legs, to touch me better.

I'd like Him to kiss me but He doesn't.

I'd like to feel His fingers on my skin but He doesn't touch me.

He stands, pulling me up with Him.

The dress slides back down my legs.

I look at Him.

He isn't looking into my eyes, but much lower.

Again very slowly, He slides the silk up over my legs,
my hips, my waist, my back, my shoulders. I lift my arms
and the dress falls to the ground.

I stay where I am, teetering on my stiletto heels, in my
garter belt and G-string and bra, all the same matte black
color, and feel more and more lost and more and more
His. I don't like my body. It's too full, too round.

His eyes linger on my skin, unsettling me and arousing me.

I hear His breathing.

"You're gorgeous."

I smile.

He takes my right hand in His and circles my waist with
his other hand and turns me around, as if in a slow waltz.

I know He's giving me the once-over.

I know how beautiful His wife is, how tall and skinny. I
saw her once at the Brasserie Lipp, but He doesn't know
that. I lower my eyes.

Silence. Not a word from Him. I can't even hear His
breathing anymore.

Instinctively, I arch my back.

"Good," He says.

◆ ◆ ◆

I'm shaking.

He sits down and looks at me in silence.

Finally I see Him undo His tie. A black tie, thin and silky.

I take this to mean that He's going to undress. It's like a return to reality. I imagine His skin, how dark and soft and smooth it must be.

But He doesn't undress. He plays with His tie, sliding it between His fingers. He smiles at me. At last, He speaks.

"Nobody has ever treated you as I'm going to treat you."

He moves His hands up toward my face. I wait for Him to stroke me. Instead, the tie goes over my eyes. I hear the silk rustle as He knots it behind my neck.

I'm shaking.

I'd like Him to kiss me but He doesn't.

I can't see a thing and I'm shaking.

I hear Him step back.

I'm lost, alone in this room I don't know, blind.

I'm shaking. He doesn't say a word.

I don't hear Him moving.

I don't know where He is now.

But I feel His eyes staring at my body.

I try to imagine what He's seeing, what He's thinking.

I see again my arched back above my excessively high, excessively pointed stilettos, reflected in the mirror of the lingerie shop near my office, where I rushed a few hours ago, anxious to follow His instructions: "Go home and prepare your body for me. Oil yourself. All over. Dress in black, with stockings and high-heeled shoes."

I'm shaking. The blindness makes my senses ten times sharper. I feel a mixture of fear and desire.

He's moving! I hear Him moving. I really think He's coming closer to me.

I stretch out my right hand to where I think He is.

His voice stops me.

"No."

My hand freezes in midair.

"Hands behind your back."

I put my palms together against the small of my back, twisting and untwisting my fingers.

I've obeyed at once, without thinking.

"That's good. You're beautiful like that."

At last, I feel His hand on me, brushing against the back of my neck, stroking it, moving down again to my breasts, which are barely held within my plunging bra.

He moves the material aside and takes my left breast in his open hand and pulls it out. Then he does the same with my right breast.

I'm conscious of my breasts rising toward Him, my nipples lifted toward His face, straining, demanding His fingers.

Now He lets go of me again and I feel lost.

I have a fierce desire to feel Him against me but I don't dare move.

When I hear His steps moving away, I feel as if I'm going to faint.

My whole body aches for His presence. There's a knot of pain in my stomach. I arch my back, as if that could grab His attention.

I hear Him breathing. He's much taller than me. I feel His breath on my forehead.

"Show me your tongue."

I don't understand. Timidly, I stick my tongue out a little, holding it tight between my teeth.

What must I look like? I promise myself to check—as soon as I can.

"A bit more."

I do as I'm told. I'm shaking.

Desire floods through me.

His tongue touches my tongue and He takes it into His mouth and His arms go around my shoulders and I abandon myself and kiss Him and suck His saliva and gorge myself on His mouth and kiss Him and kiss Him and kiss Him and my head explodes and I stagger, my legs buckling under the intensity of the desire going through my body.

I'm not shaking anymore, my hands are responding, I hug Him as hard as I can and stroke His face, guessing at the contours, I cling to Him with all the passion I have in me, as if my body could be absorbed by His.

But already His mouth is leaving my mouth, His body rejecting my body.

I stay where I am, struggling against the spasms that shudder through me. I can't bear not being able to see Him, not having Him near me, my mouth and belly and back are aching for His hands, screaming their sense of abandonment, demanding His touch, His voice, His smell. But I don't make a sound.

He doesn't speak to me, doesn't approach me, doesn't touch me.

◆ ◆ ◆

After what seems an infinite length of time, I finally feel His hands on my shoulders. He grips them and pushes me backward, until I feel a table behind my thighs.

I grip the edge of the table, which seems to be of polished wood.

He rearranges the position of my breasts, pulling back the cups of the bra as far as they will go.

I feel His fingers on my nipples, then His mouth biting them, His fingers pinching them with increasing strength, His tongue licking them, His lips exploring them and sucking on them, I feel His teeth squeezing and biting me more and more greedily. I'm shaking more than ever, heat rises in the small of my back. I arch my back even more. My belly is on fire, too.

His teeth and tongue and fingers work away, sometimes gently, sometimes painfully. My head is exploding.

All I want is to be fucked by this man I know nothing about, this man who's treating me as nobody has ever treated me.

He lets go of me. I support myself on the table.

"Nobody will ever treat you as I'm going to treat you." A grim omen.

◆ ◆ ◆

"Turn."

I turn.

"Arch your back."

I arch my back.

"Spread your buttocks."

I stop moving.

I feel His hands on my hands, which are still clamped on the table.

With infinite gentleness this time, His fingers intertwine with mine.

With my hands still in His, He places them on my buttocks, one on each side of my ass.

He spreads my buttocks and I feel His sinuous tongue licking me, cutting a path deep inside me.

I want to turn and suck Him, but I know it's not the right moment.

The shaking starts again.

He kneels and puts His face against my buttocks, His thumb takes over from His tongue, then another finger, then His tongue again. His breathing is labored and spasmodic.

The phone rings, making me jump.

He stops, and I hear His steps in the room.

The soles of His shoes click on the parquet floor—a clear indication that He's still dressed.

◆ ◆ ◆

"Helen? My meeting hasn't finished yet. I'll meet you as soon as I'm done.

"Arch your back."

I realize He's talking to me. Did she hear? I arch my back.

"See you soon, darling." (Will He call me "darling" one day?)

I hear His steps in the room, a drawer opening and closing. He's behind me again, parting my hair at the back. I tremble when he runs His nails over the nape of my neck.

"Concentrate on what I'm going to do to you. I'm going to drive you crazy. You'll never again be able to do without it. You'll wait for me to call you, you'll pray for me to send for you, you'll come right away and do everything I ask. You'll learn to enjoy waiting for me, needing me. You'll never again have an orgasm without thinking of me. You'll never again have an orgasm without thinking of this."

I'm overcome with emotion.

The tie is coming loose and about to slide from my eyes. He tightens the knot.

◆ ◆ ◆

Again, He searches in my ass with his fingers. "Masturbate." I find my clitoris with my middle finger while He continues His exploration, right and left, up and down. I'm shaking, my orgasm is mounting. I'm going to come, but He lets go of my hand and turns me to face Him and puts His fingers on my lips.

"Lick them, suck them, think about what I'm going to do to you."

One by one, I lick and suck the fingers He's just taken out of my ass.

"Go on, that's good, you're very submissive. I like that."

My tongue penetrates every fold of His skin, I take His thumb into my mouth, and I can't stop thinking about His cock, I'd like to feel it inside me, no matter where, no matter how, as long as it's right now. After I've cleaned every nook and cranny of His skin with my tongue, He turns me around again to face the table, presses my face onto the wood, my nose squashed against the lacquer. I hear the noise of a tube emptying into my anus.

I realize He's going to sodomize me and I wait for His cock.

Anticipating His orders, I arch my back.

◆ ◆ ◆

"Get ready. Open wide."

I obey. Something hard and pointed forces its way through my sphincter and plunges into me.

It can't be His cock. It doesn't hurt.

The unidentified object moves backward and forward, impaling me.

The thing is very long, and I feel as if it's going to pierce my intestines.

A pencil? No, it's much thicker than a pencil. A letter opener, a stick? I don't know, I'll never know.

Whatever it is, He takes it out and again I feel a thick finger going in. Is it His thumb? He turns it a little in my dampened ass.

Then nothing.

The top half of my body is still flat across the table and my hands twist beneath my face. I bite my fingers in order not to cry out.

"Don't move."

He didn't need to say it. I wouldn't have moved. I'd never have dared to move.

This time, something much wider forces its way into my ass, and by now, I have to admit, there isn't much resistance.

I think it's His cock and arch my back even more. I

close my eyes and hold my breath to savor the feel of Him at last inside me.

My senses have deceived me. No sooner has my ass been filled than He lifts the top part of my body and turns me to face Him again. The thing is still inside me. I can't get over it. I'm torn in two but I know He's in front of me.

"You're a bit narrow. I need to make you wider."

He puts His mouth on mine and bites my lips. His kisses make me dizzy.

I'm totally submissive, abandoned, malleable. I already know He could do anything He wants to me, I'd follow Him anywhere, I'd go with Him to a cloister and devote myself to serving Him, giving Him pleasure, obeying Him. All I can think about is the thing inside me.

I'm on my feet again now, so why hasn't it slipped out? What is it? It doesn't really hurt, it's just there. I can't work out its shape or what it's made of. But I'd rather die than ask Him.

Now He grabs my hips with His hands and lifts me up till I'm sitting on the table. Of course I don't dare put my weight on my anus and what's in it. Instead, I try to support myself on my thighs.

I hear the sound of furniture being moved. "Open your legs."

"Put your feet on the chairs," and at the same time, He places one of my legs on a chair to the right of my body, then the other the same way, on the other side.

With my thighs as far apart as they can go, I'm forced to shift my weight backward.

The thing sinks into me.

I can't see how it's possible, and I've no idea how He plans to get it out. The prospect overwhelms me. Again, I'm shaking all over.

"That's good, you needed widening. Lean on it. Butt-fuck yourself."

I clutch the edge of the table on either side of my legs and try to shift a little of my weight onto my hands.

"Hands behind your back."

I fear the worst, but I don't dare disobey Him. I join my hands behind my back, still trying to lean on them.

"You're making fun of me!"

He grabs a mass of hair behind my neck and pulls it down. My weight shifts completely onto my coccyx and the thing goes even farther in.

◆ ◆ ◆

Something brushes against my hip. It feels like a rather thick cloth. He grabs my hands and ties my wrists with the cloth and pulls the knot very tight.

I lower my head. I'm shaking.

The blindfold has become a little loose. Between my thighs, I can see His hips in His black suit. My ass hurts. I think about torture by impalement. God knows how this is going to end.

I feel as if my tissues are tearing. All my weight now is on the thing, which seems more and more enormous.

I watch Him through my restricted field of vision. I want to cry. The thing is completely inside me now. I want Him to untie me and turn me around and at least reassure me that He'll be able to take it out. I want His cock. I want to make Him come.

There's total silence. I can't see His face but I sense that He's looking at me. I breathe faster.

His black suit reappears in the crack. His jacket is open and I notice He's wearing a belt with a silver buckle. His shirt is white, with what look like very thin blue stripes— I can hardly see anything. The belt disappears. I see nothing but white, then His face, then His hair.

He moves aside my panties and lightly touches my cunt and sticks His forefinger inside, then takes it out and raises it to my mouth. "You're soaking wet." I suck His damp finger.

All I can see now is His dark, stiff hair, brushed back.

And I feel His tongue in me and His nose burrows into my pubis and His lips suck on my clitoris, His tongue is tender and rough, it edges its way in, burrows into my body, and His fingers are in there, too, moving with increasing force, and with small and then bigger flicks of His tongue. He climbs and sucks and teases and stops and starts again, with the precision of a bullet reaching its target.

My ass hurts. The bonds cut into my wrists. My cunt reaches the point of ecstasy and explodes. Convulsions shake my body and I bite my lips so as not to cry out.

I'm drowning in the ocean, lights flash before my eyes. I'm dying. The orgasm is incredible, overwhelming, the spasms go on and on.

I haven't touched Him. My hands are tied. I can't even hug Him.

Long seconds pass. He's still between my legs. He's put His hand on my erupting cunt and His cheek against my left thigh.

He stands up and kisses me. I drink my own juice greedily, putting into my kiss all the gratitude I feel for this unfamiliar power.

He lifts me off the table and takes the thing out of me (I'll never know how) and unties me and kisses me again and takes off the blindfold.

"I'll see you soon," He says as He walks me to the door. "Don't call me. I'll send for you when I want to see you again." And that's it.

Now I'm back in the street, walking beside the railings of the Luxembourg, my head full of Him, already waiting for His call.

II

Every day that passes is like a blade plunging that much farther into my body, that much closer to my heart.

I keep my cell phone with me all the time, avidly check the list of the calls that come in to my office, tremble every time a private number flashes up.

But it isn't Him. It's never Him.

In the meantime, I've resumed a strict diet based on appetite suppressants. The needle on my scales veering ever farther to the left is a great consolation.

Whenever I'm alone, in my car, on my horse, in church, I recall His skin, and try to remember the tone of His voice, His words, His hands on me.

◆ ◆ ◆

I can't get to sleep at night without imagining His fingers on my skin and His cock and His whispered orders. With every day that passes, the memory of His voice fades a little more.

Every morning, I get ready, hoping He'll send for me today. I wear only skirts or dresses now, with stockings. I've hidden my high-heeled shoes behind a pile of files in a cabinet in my office.

But He doesn't call me.

Every day my desire to see Him grows stronger, but so does the likelihood that He's forgotten me. The pain of it is unbearable.

I have a terrible sense of waste, of something unfinished. So much to experience, so much to give, if only He knew. I need to see Him again, to show Him I can be worthy of him, to pay tribute to him, make Him proud of me, devote myself to His pleasure. He can do what He wants with me, with my body and my soul, I can rise to His demands, all I'm waiting for are His orders, all I need is one word from Him.

Why doesn't He call?

He doesn't even know me. He wouldn't recognize my voice, maybe just my arched back, which is waiting for him, begging for Him to do what He will with me.

I'd like to be able to tell Him that I expect nothing of Him, that all I want is to be a steamy episode in His unavoidable routine.

The torture of waiting.

I can't get over it. Waiting for Him to want me one day, I'll be so good to Him, I'll give Him a hard-on. He didn't give me time, I couldn't show Him, I didn't know how. If only He knew what I'm capable of, how racked with desire I am, how submissive I'll be, defying all the rules and conventions, giving myself to Him totally.

I can't sleep now without thinking about Him, I can't come without thinking about what He did to me. I think about it all the time. Although I lead a wonderful life, sur-rounded by a family and friends I can count on, and lucky to handle fascinating cases that bring me money and grat-itude from my clients, I feel His absence, all I think about is starting again and this time going further, setting out across the desert, satisfying desires I didn't know I had, opening the gates to cities of depravity I already know I can't do without.

How did He know I'd come when He called?

Why has He abandoned me after giving me a taste of His smell and His tongue and His skin? I want to know His cock,

support Him in His perversions, feast on bitter fruit, antici-
pate His desires, go further than He's even dreamed of.

Time passes and the pain of the memory gets worse. I
don't even dare talk about it to Bérénice, my best friend
and closest confidante. I feel alone, more alone than I've
ever been. I watch my son playing, and avoid the glances
my husband throws me.

I met my husband when I was very young, it was he
who molded me, made me the woman I am. He's so often
put his arms around me and assured me of his support
and convinced me he was the man, the only man for me.
I've never cheated on him, never needed to lie to him.

And now, as if suddenly caught in an unexpected storm, I
even forget my own name, all I do is wait and wait for a
sign from someone else, a man who didn't even fuck me,
didn't even possess me, I'm haunted by a fleeting pleasure, an unforgettable, unequaled pleasure, His breath on
my skin, His words against my forehead. Sometimes I
close my eyes and imagine I could go back in time and
wipe it out and become an ideal wife and mother again.
How can a few hours reverse the meaning of a whole life-
time? I know I'll never again be the same as I was before,
and that if I had to do it again, I would. I hug my husband, who's back from the goddamn Far East, and whis-

per that I love him, that I'm his, and I wish I believed it, I wish I still believed it, I wish I could remove the knife I have inside me, the knife that is killing my innocence, but he doesn't know that and I can't tell him, can't ask him to look after me, not this time, he wouldn't understand, nobody would understand, I'm standing alone on the edge of a precipice waiting for the devil to push me into the abyss, wanting nothing but to start again, even if it means the destruction of all the things I hold dear.

I wish I could go to bed and sleep and get up and dress and go to work and not think about it, I wish I could laugh about the whole thing, store the episode away in a closet of memories like my first boyfriend's letters. I wish I could forget the strange pleasure of pain and submission, the spasms, my hungry cunt crying out to be filled. I wish I could forget the desire to have that unknown, arrogant cock inside me. I wish I could stop imagining how my flesh would stroke it, massage it, moving up and down, contracting, gradually getting stronger, how my vagina would tame it and suck it, how my mucous membranes would taste it and sniff it and stroke it. I wish I could give up the idea of wrapping it deep inside me, as far as it'll go, savoring every particle, every inch of that cock. But I can't because I haven't had that cock and it's all I can think about.

◆ ◆ ◆

I can't close my eyes now without remembering the first time He looked at me, in court, the moment He turned to the public after swaying the jury, that woman crying, the heinous nature of the crime, His bloodshot gray eyes, the brilliance of His words, the strength of His body.

The way I lowered my eyes when I had to stand up and speak after Him, so shaken by the unassailable power of His speech I was at a loss for words.

The way He came up to me, after the verdict was announced and His client was acquitted, and said, "I'll call you, I have something to tell you," and I stammered an almost inaudible "Yes." Did I already know? That was the first promise He didn't keep. I didn't know Him and already I was waiting to hear His voice.

Weeks later, His voice on my answering machine, the unexpected, inexplicable excitement I felt at the thought of seeing Him again. Why Him, and not any of the men I meet at dinners, or at the Palais de Justice, or at the race track, the men I seduce with a laugh, a clever piece of repartee, a bold display of horsemanship? I've always been lucky enough to choose, to call the shots, to leave when I want to, and now I'm stuck with the emptiness, the unbearable pain, of a man's indifference.

◆ ◆ ◆

I look at my husband and hug my son and don't understand myself anymore, I feel bewitched, obsessed, desperate.

The phone rings and it isn't Him. I don't understand. "Don't call me," He said. "I'll send for you."

After Him, nothing and nobody is worth it. I know I'll never again experience anything as intense with anyone else.

I don't want a lover. He isn't a lover.

III

By the time I get to the Montalembert, there's a knot in my stomach. It's the first time I've ever used a hotel in Paris, because I've never cheated on my husband. Why risk causing suffering and losing everything, and all for what? A strange man getting dressed in a hurry, embarrassed and disgusted after "making love" to me, after filling my body, and me wanting nothing more than to forget the moans that remain like a stain on my conscience.

But now I go to the reception desk and ask for His room, exactly as He asked, without any hesitation. These are the first moves in a game—I don't know the rules, but I accept them in advance.

◆ ◆ ◆

Maybe that's submission.

The desk clerk smiles courteously and tells me the key to Room 17 is already in the door. He offers to accompany me, but I politely decline. I walk through the hotel as if in a dream, my steps guided by a kind of inner force, an unassailable impulse, a subversive desire. I adjust my stockings and check that my breasts fit snugly in my half-cup bra.

I knock at the door of the room. He doesn't answer. I tremble as I turn the key in the lock and push open the heavy wooden door, which creaks as it swings on its hinges.

The room is dark. The purple velvet curtains are closed. I look for the light switch. The pink porcelain Chinese bedside lamps come on. There's a big bed in the middle of the room. The bedspread is chintz, with a pattern of roses and sweetbriar. On the bed, a rectangular white cardboard box and an envelope. I have cramps in my stomach. I look around me, barely able to breathe. He's not here.

Just the box and the envelope.

I walk forward, my steps muffled by the carpet. On a little round glass table, a bottle of champagne is waiting in an ice bucket. Purple roses fill the room with their fragrance.

◆ ◆ ◆

I'm surprised by such exquisite refinement, such thought-fulness. I've been dreading something seedier.

My steps still muffled, as if I'm walking in a temple, I continue my exploration, all the while listening closely for Him. I go to a door on the other side of the bed and find myself in a huge bathroom, with gray marble walls and floor, a big corner bath, a shower stall, and a sink.

But He isn't there. I whisper His name, then go back to the bedroom and sit down on the bed and pick up the envelope. On the top, scribbled in pencil: *To Élodie, by hand.*

I close my eyes for a moment. The only sound is my heart, which is beating so hard it could burst. I tear the envelope with trembling fingers and, as I read the letter it contains, my eyes mist over.

> *Élodie, I want you to observe the following instructions to the letter.*
> *1) Open the box on the bed*
> *2) Put on the clothes that are inside*
> *3) Put the toy inside you*
> *4) Put on the blindfold*
> *5) Kneel on the bed, with your back to the door, and wait for me*

*If for any reason I discover when I arrive that
you've disobeyed any of these commands, I'll con-
sider you unworthy of me. But I know you'll obey.
See you soon.*

I sit there without moving, unable to put the letter down,
and try to regain my composure.

Never in a million years could I have imagined that one
day I would be in this situation, ready to submit to the
most outlandish demands from a man I know nothing
about, a man I hardly know, who treats me in such an off-
hand way, and yet feel such intense excitement.

It's several minutes before I pick up the box. It's quite a
big box, made of grainy white cardboard, and tied with a
black ribbon. There's nothing written on it.

I pull on the bow. The ribbon slides through my fingers. I
hold my breath as I lift the lid and tear the gray tissue
paper. I don't dare look inside. I slide something out of
the box: it's a black latex leotard, with two big round
openings on the chest and a long zipper in the back.

I smile, thinking of the money I blew at Sabbia Rosa
because I wanted to be equal to the occasion.

I put the leotard down on the bed and look in the box

again. I find a garter belt of the same material and a pair of fishnet stockings.

My stomach tenses up again. I stand up and stagger to the bathroom, where I get out of my new dress and slip into the leotard. The latex crackles beneath my fingers and sticks to my skin. As I put it on, I notice there's a slit, some six inches long, between the thighs. Obviously.

I refuse to think about what I'm doing.

Not for a moment does it occur to me to escape, not for a second do I think about my son, my life. It just doesn't occur to me to leave this hotel, which symbolizes everything I think I'm not, and run away.

The image of me reflected in the bathroom mirrors is astounding: the G-string cuts into my skin, the leotard is very tight, and the openings at the front make it tighter across my lower back.

I slide the stockings over my legs and attach them at the top of my thighs.

I put on my favorite shoes (the ones I wore the first time) and look at the young woman in the mirror. I find it hard

to identify with her. She looks more like the heroine of an
S&M movie than a girl from a convent school. I laugh
nervously. How have I gotten to this point?

I remember the other instructions. I walk back nervously
to the bedroom to see what else, what other "accessories,"
He's got for me in the box.

At the bottom of the box, a black Lycra blindfold and a
length of string with three steel balls threaded through it,
each the size of a golf ball, a little over an inch apart.
Surprised, I study the object, turning it between my fingers. The balls are smooth and cold.

I reread the "letter" several times, puzzled by the third
instruction: *Put the toy inside you.* So that's it, these must
be the famous "geisha balls"! I laugh at my own innocence—until I realize that what I have to do is push them
inside me through the slit in the body stocking, which I'm
finding increasingly irritating. But I have to do it. There's
no way I'm going to fail in my duty. I push the first ball into
my cunt. The contact of the icy steel is a bit of a shock. The
ball is too big. It's hard, maybe even impossible, to get in.
Stretched out on the bed, with my legs open, I try to push
this foreign body inside me. I've already been in this room
for twenty minutes. I'm terrified that He might get here
before I'm ready. But my cunt resists.

I close my eyes and touch myself and think about Him, and at last my cunt begins to respond.

I push the first ball in as hard as I can, and this time my vagina obeys.

It's strange to feel this cold thing inside me, there's even something a little bit pleasurable about it.

After the first one, the others follow without too much difficulty. Quite proud of myself, I put on the blindfold. I'm ready for Him.

I lie there on the bed, unable to see, and, for the umpteenth time in forty-four days, remember His voice, which I haven't heard again, and His skin, which I haven't touched again. I know He'll come, I know He knows I'm waiting, I try to imagine what He's thinking about at this very moment, where He is, how fast or slow He's walking, what He's going to ask me, what He's going to do to me.

With the geisha balls inside me, so cold and strange, I realize for the first time how powerful, how irresistible the desire of the mind is.

I need His words, His commands. How did He know I'd respond to Him? How did He recognize me? How did He know I was capable of following him? The questions nag at me. My husband's position, my classic suits, my lawyer's robes, my business card, my bourgeois manners: none of these things seems to hold out much promise of extreme depravity. Does He treat all the women who pass through His hands in the same way? Do the others also enjoy being submissive? I think about my girlfriends, my dear girlfriends. I know so many of their deepest secrets, if only I could tell them, if only they could understand the irresistible attraction, the unforgivable impulse, the joy of being a slave, of wallowing in desire for a man who's a God and a devil, worshiping Him, bowing down before Him and waiting for a sign, a word, a breath, anything to reawaken your sleeping senses!

And why don't all these men around me in this world of mine know what we're waiting for? Why don't they have the courage to talk to us and tell us things that surprise us and leave us in suspense? Why don't they know what we desire, even if we don't know it ourselves? Why don't they take our souls and our lives and transform us into greedy animals, degraded and submissive, begging for a few commands, a few words, a few challenges, which would make us quiver and realize that nothing else existed before this? Why don't they understand that the mechanical couplings we've all had to submit to are as nothing compared with how it feels to give ourselves, to

surrender and forget about everything except being worthy, being equal to the demands of the God who's made us
His? Why don't they understand the power of fantasy? It's
fantasy that increases tenfold the pleasure of an orgasm,
it's words that drive us crazy.

The balls are bothering me. They really are big. He knows
it, He knows I'm waiting, I've been waiting for forty-four
hours and can't stand any more waiting, not a minute goes
by that I don't think about Him. He's going to arrive, He's
going to open the door, and I won't even see Him.

My eyes closed behind the blindfold, I dream of His hands
on me.

All at once, I realize time's passed and I've *forgotten* his
fifth commandment: *Kneel on the bed, with your back to
the door, and wait for me.* My eyes are covered. I can't
read the letter unless I take the blindfold off, but I can't
do that—not that that's any excuse.

   I turn around. I'm in despair. How could I? How long
have I been here? How long did I spend in the bathroom,
trying to fit into this body stocking, which is so tight and
so uncomfortable? Why isn't He here? Maybe He came in
without my hearing Him and I wasn't ready and He saw
me here, lying peacefully on the bed, not even capable of

doing the simplest thing: getting ready and turning my back and waiting for Him because I'm His and He does me the honor of telling me exactly what He expects of me, it's all so simple.

I don't understand. I don't understand anything anymore. What time is it? Why isn't He here? He can't not come. Will He still come, or come back, if by chance he's already been here? Will He agree to give me a second chance? I find that so hard to imagine. But what if He's already here? He might have come in, and I didn't hear Him. He's looking at me in silence, He's been looking at me for some time, but for how long? Speak His name, call Him, but I'm not allowed. Maybe that's the point of today: silence, the absence of words, the absence of touch. He's here, looking at me and savoring the fact that I don't know He's here, savoring the fact that I'm here in this room for Him, only for Him.

Time passes. My tense, arched body no longer belongs to me. I feel ill. Cramps, backache. My vagina, full of something that isn't Him, is rebelling.

I collapse, exhausted, and dare to look at my watch. It's nearly a quarter to six. I tear off the blindfold. It's wet with my tears and sticks to my face. I get dressed. I feel so ill all of a sudden. What am I supposed to do with His toys?

In a daze, I put them back in the box and give them to the hotel porter and run off without a word, out into the street, where I cry, alone. I feel as though I've spoiled everything.

He calls me seventeen days later, to tell me He couldn't join me at the Montalembert because He was held up, and to thank me for leaving His "things," I could have kept them, He'd have happily lent them to me, because He checked how long I waited and what time I left and I really deserved them.

Maybe He'll have some free time next Wednesday. He'll call me.

IV

Once again I'm waiting desperately for Him to call. I sit staring at my phone and have to stop myself from dialing the number of His law firm.

What would I say to Him? "You said you'd call, I've waited too long, I have to see you. I can't wait anymore, I have so much to offer you, you haven't let me show you, let me try, maybe I'd be able to give you an erection, maybe I'd make you want me, if only you knew how I dream about you in bed at night, your hands on me, your cock inside me, give me a chance."

That's absurd. It's up to Him to call me. What's the point of telling a man without desire about my desire for Him? If He wanted to see me, He'd say so.

———◆———

My secretary tells me He's on the phone and wants to talk to me. I barely have time to regain my composure before I hear His voice: "I've missed you a lot. You should have called me, these last few weeks have been so hard. I was waiting for a sign from you."

I must be dreaming. He's making fun of me, but I don't contradict Him.

He wants to see me. As soon as possible. He demands that I make myself available the day after tomorrow, "Thursday evening."

I go through my wardrobe in my mind, my underwear, my shoes.

I have to choose the stockings, the garter belt, the bustier: tulle or lace?

I return home and my son holds out his arms to me. I'm moved but I don't linger. I love him more than anything in the world but he's not enough for me.

I'm dreaming with my eyes open, preparing my body, making it smooth and glossy, exfoliating, plucking, and taking Ambien to get to sleep.

◆ ◆ ◆

The day arrives, and I wake up with a start, at dawn. I've been dreaming about Him all night. Like the other nights. Except that tonight, I know I'll be in His hands. Tonight.

I'm afraid. I'm paralyzed with impatience. I know I'm ready for anything. I'd like to know my limits.

I drink my usual two quarts of tea, but do without my daily sliced bread with salted butter and black cherry jam. I don't look at my husband. My son is still asleep when I slam the door shut behind me. I don't want to hear his gurgles.

My stomach feels bad again. It's anxiety, I suppose.

By the time I arrive at my firm, my face is wreathed in smiles. None of my cases can take them away.

My period has started. I cry with rage. There's nothing I can do. Even if I stuff myself full of Methergin to control the bleeding, I can't take the risk. I feel so ashamed. I just can't believe it. I have to call Him. But what can I say? What can I suggest?

While I'm struggling with this insoluble problem, Léon, an old friend of mine and a past master at seduction, calls me to invite us to dinner next Tuesday.

I gladly accept.

The thing that's special about his dinners is that he always invites a lot of unusual and eccentric people. This one, which is being organized by his wife, the incredible Astrid, looks like it's sure to be a colorful affair. The guests include a falsely modest philosopher who wrote an encyclopedia all on his own; my mysterious colleague Hassan with his fine features and his dark skin, who's envied by half the lawyers in Paris for his women and his high media profile and who makes the other half (the female half) jealous for the same reasons, and a well-known sexologist whose reputation probably owes a lot to the special care he lavishes on his female patients, and who'll be there with his girlfriend, a model and actress with an extraordinarily sensual mouth. Who else? There's a financier who, after a few setbacks in the stock market, thinks the whole town has it in for him; his wife, a pretty fortysomething who has nothing to recommend her except her family jewels; a few ultrarespectable company directors whose daughters are all called Marie something or other; a specialist in face-lifts for very rich and very neurotic women; and a pretty woman in her forties who finds it impossible to choose between her husband and her lover. There's Aurélien, whom everyone is attracted to, and who seduced my dear friend, the lovely Léa, on the eve of her nineteenth birthday—three years later she still has a glint in her eyes when she talks about him. There's a woman director of erotic neorealist films; an ambassador who knows my husband well; Bérénice, who's absolutely my best friend, the most loyal, the most reliable, but whom I still can't tell, plus a few others who are well accepted in polite society—and Him!

When I hear His name, my heart skips a beat.

I knew they were friends. In fact, I'd already met Him at Léon's, but now my heart starts racing again, the excitement is unbearable—all these friends, my husband, Him, and me.

I thank Léon, tell him I'll definitely be there, and quickly hang up. I immediately dial the number of His law firm.

Without preparing what I'm going to say, I plunge in: "I'm really sorry, I can't make it tomorrow evening. But I think we'll see each other at Léon's dinner next Tuesday. Anyway, I thought maybe you'd like to meet after the dinner, maybe Wednesday evening. The whole of Tuesday evening we'll be having dinner together with mutual friends, both knowing I'll be yours the next day."

"Yes. All right. Bye, then."

That's all. He's already hung up.

I'm overexcited. Everything's churning inside me. I'm very proud that I managed to speak to Him without stammering, and I even convince myself that I could call Him again next Monday to ask if He'd like to go with me to choose the underwear I'll be wearing on Tuesday evening. Only He would know.

On Monday morning, I wait impatiently until eleven o'clock, when I think I'm more likely to find Him in His office. In the end, I have to leave a message. Then I wait.

The hours pass. As soon as I leave my office, I switch all incoming calls to my secretarial staff.

At last, at seven o'clock, He phones. I immediately make my suggestion, which he accepts without much enthusiasm. Appointment at twelve o'clock tomorrow, at La Perla.

I decide I won't eat till then. It's not hard to do.

◆ ◆ ◆

Tuesday. At 11:58, I'm stuck in a massive traffic jam in the place de la Concorde. To think that I left my scooter behind this morning so that I'd be impeccable in my favorite gear: stilettos and stockings and garters. And now I'm definitely late.

◆

At 12:28, I park, blocking a driveway opposite La Perla, and run into the shop. He isn't there. The assistant—who's very unpleasant—tells me He waited for me, but left five minutes ago.

My eyes fill with tears. I'm desperate. My legs won't carry me anymore.

I stand there in my stilettos, in the boulevard Saint-Germain, and look down at the sidewalk, feeling hopeless. I cross the street, narrowly avoiding being run over. The drivers blow their horns noisily to show their disapproval, or maybe to jolt me out of my torpor.

Staring into space, I light a cigarette and smoke it and walk aimlessly like a zombie.

Suddenly I see Him. He's just a few yards away, sitting on the terrace of the Flore. I quickly join Him, summoning all my energy to put on a bold front.

◆ ◆ ◆

"You're late."

It's true. I lower my eyes and mutter some inaudible excuses.

"This is quite unacceptable. If it wasn't for the fact that I have an appointment with a journalist at one o'clock, I'd take you home with me and punish you."

I don't say anything. I want Him, maybe I also want Him to punish me.

I'm transported by His voice as He tells me I'm His, He can do what he wants with me, He likes my sensuality and my submissiveness. He'll look at me tonight and think about His hands on my breasts, the smell of my cunt, His tongue in my ass. He'll want to tie my hands and take me behind a column. He'll want to fuck me. He'll want me to suck Him.

He tells me that when I go home, I'll think about Him and masturbate.

He tells me I look beautiful in my severe navy blue suit, He can see from the glances of other men how much I'm desired, but only He knows how submissive I am, how ready to carry out all His orders.

He talks about Catherine Millet.

Although I admire her sincerity, the endless succession of penetrations she describes isn't my kind of fantasy at all.

◆ ◆ ◆

He takes me by the arm and we go into L'Écume des Pages, where He buys me *Dolorosa Soror* by Florence Dugas and *Le Lien* by Vanessa Duries.

"These books could have been written for you," He says as He hands them to me. "Maybe one day you'll feel the need to write about your experiences with me."

He walks me to my car and opens the door for me. I'm just about to drive off when He asks: "How did your riding competition go on Sunday?"

I'm astonished He remembers about this event since we hardly touched on it during our short conversations these last few days.

"Um, very well, thanks, I came in third in the jumping."

"Do you carry a whip when you ride?"

"A riding crop? Yes, but I never use it, my mare's so good—"

"What's the whip like?"

"Uh, black."

"Tonight, I want you to leave it in the hall of Léon's building, under the stairs. You were late today. You have to be punished."

And He's gone.

His last words have left me stunned. I rush to the riding department at Hermès to buy a whip worthy of Him.

Obviously, I couldn't give Him the old piece of plastic I've had hanging around in my tack room for the last ten years.

I choose a black latticework leather cane, with a broad lash. I don't know if the clerk has guessed what I'm planning to use it for, but from his questions he sounds suspicious.

"Is it for you? Are you jumping? If you are, there's no point in buying something so beautiful, this one's cheaper and better suited from a technical point of view."

What business is it of his?

I try to put him off the scent by making him show me all the bits he has in stock—the only one missing, of course, is the one that would fit my mare's mouth—just to prove to this jumped-up idiot that I really do ride. All the same, I don't know if I'll ever get this thing out of here without stammering.

"Th-thanks. I told you it was for me! No need to gift-wrap it!"

I promise myself that next time I'll prepare myself in advance by going to buy some lubricant at the drugstore below my office.

—◆—

At last, I throw the whip on the backseat and drive back to work. But I don't work, just try to think of the most discreet way to hide the thing in Léon's hall without anyone noticing—especially with my husband there.

In the end, it all happens without fuss. As usual, I'm late, trying to decide what to wear: my figure-hugging black Versace dress, which is a bit short, the Prada suit Léa has lent me, or my black leather skirt with the slit up the side, which has the disadvantage of showing the top of my stockings. In the end, I opt for the Prada suit.

In the meantime, my husband has lost patience and left in the car, telling me to join him as soon as possible.

If only he knew how grateful I am to him!

About twenty minutes later, I emerge from the taxi at the quai de Béthune with the whip concealed inside my bustier, making sure first that nobody else has just arrived. I'm shaking.

I don't have much time to hide the thing. Every second counts. But I'm still standing undecided in the entrance hall with the whip in my hands, looking at the front door, the steps, the pedestal table, when I hear the door opening behind me.

I immediately throw the whip, with its promise of pain, into a baby's stroller, take a deep breath, try to regain my composure, and walk into Léon's apartment. I look around the group. He isn't here.

I immediately drown myself in champagne.

Time passes and He still isn't here. What if He doesn't come? I think of the hours I waited at the Montalembert. How can I retrieve the whip?

Trying to look as natural as possible, I keep my eyes trained on the door, watching out for His tall figure.

Almost ten o'clock and still nothing. Everyone else is here except Him.

One of the guests hands me a huge joint. I inhale deeply. Once. Twice. Three times.

I feel sick. I want to vomit, I want to laugh, I want to cry. At moments, my mind goes blank and I wonder where I am.

I feel ill. I sit down on the floor at Léon's feet, my knees bent under me, and laugh like an idiot and really don't feel well.

And then I see Him. He's sitting opposite me, watching me. I don't know if what I see in His eyes is disdain or amusement. He came in without my noticing and sat down opposite me, and I don't know how long He's been watching me.

I try to get a grip on myself and control my ridiculous giggling.

I put down my glass and take a deep breath to regain my composure. I have a nasty feeling everyone here can see how flustered I am. In addition to which, my husband's looking at me and it's clear he isn't pleased at all. I lower my eyes, unable to sustain his gaze.

As for Him, He's talking to Léon and not taking any notice of me. He didn't even kiss me when He came in, didn't even say hello.

I feel alone in the middle of all these friends.

I feel like running away but I can't move. Then, with great effort, I get to my feet and go to freshen up.

As I come out of the toilet, I feel a hand on my hip and He pushes me toward the staircase leading downstairs. It's a big apartment, and there's a cellar.

I'm drunk and I'm high, both at the same time. He forces me down the stairs.

My legs falter and I almost fall.

He's behind me, with His hand over my mouth.

I feel His other hand moving up my stockings and feeling between my legs.

"You're soaking wet."

◆ ◆ ◆

I'm alive again. I feel the whole of Him against me. He's going to make use of me.

It's dark and I don't know where we are. A rope snags my ear, and instinctively I put my hand up to touch it.

It feels like a clothesline.

Behind me, He bites the back of my neck. I moan, but He puts His hand over my mouth to stifle the sound.

I can't see Him, all I can feel is His body against my back and His fingers burrowing in my cunt.

I want to cry out and turn around and kiss Him, but I can't because He's holding me too tight.

"You're ridiculous, completely drunk, completely stoned; next time I'll beat you till you bleed. You'll feel the sting of the whip on your hips and buttocks and back.

"You'll want to scream, but you'll be gagged.

"You'll want to cry, but you'll be blindfolded.

"You'll want to run away, but you'll be tied up.

"You'll have no way of begging me, I'll do what I want with you.

"Maybe I'll bring other men along, you'll never know who.

"Maybe I'll fuck you in the ass, the whip will be nothing compared with what you feel when I butt-fuck you, I'll plunge into you then withdraw, then plunge in again, I'll hurt you, I'll be brutal, I'll start all over again, I'll tear you apart, maybe I'll let other men have you, you'll never know if it's still me or if I'm watching you being plowed into by a man, maybe several men, men you've never seen, men you haven't chosen.

"Maybe I'll bring other girls along as well, and then I'll lift the blindfold so you can watch me fuck them.

"Nobody will ever treat you as I'm going to treat you, you'll live in fear of me leaving you.

"You'll give me your life if I want it.

"You're mine. I'm your Master.

"Every time I send for you, you'll come running, you'll be afraid it's the last time.

"You'll never rebel."

His voice is strong and solemn and hypnotic. Nobody, ever, has talked to me like Him. Nobody has ever treated me like Him.

How did He know? How did He recognize me?

Does he treat others the same way?

I'd like the earth to stop turning. I'd like to die here in this laundry room, with His voice in my head.

◆ ◆ ◆

His fingers are burrowing into me, exciting me more and more. He bites me. I'm going to come.

Just as I'm feeling the first tremors, He takes His fingers out and moves away from me and I'm so bereft I could scream.

I put my hand out to Him. He's moved back, but I manage to feel His cock. He has a hard-on. The material of his trousers is stretched to the breaking point.

"The whip will be nothing in comparison." He's warned me.

I want Him. I want to feel Him inside me. At least once. If only He'd have me. Somehow, I find the courage to whisper: "Please, take me, I beg you, fuck me."

He puts His hand back on my cunt, and my legs sag.

I suddenly feel a tremendous pain.

He's pressing my cunt very hard, I'm not sure where, but it hurts a lot.

He takes His hand away from my crotch but the pain remains.

He pushes me toward the staircase and forces me to walk up, despite the unbearable pain, which is getting worse.

Halfway up the stairs, He stops me and whispers very softly in my ear. "This is my punishment for tonight. Keep this object on you all evening. I order you not to touch it before you leave here. If you disobey me, I'll never see you again. You're free but I know you'll keep it. Now I'm going back up alone. Join me in a few minutes."

And He continues walking up to the first floor.

I collapse in the middle of the stairs, and try to regain my composure.

The pain is extreme. But it doesn't occur to me to remove what's causing it. I like the torture.

I'm going to go back upstairs and take my place among the guests and join in the conversation.

Only He will know.

The words He whispered echo in my head like a cry in a cave. I want to be His, I want Him to beat me all over, I want every inch of my skin to bear His stamp.

I want Him to mistreat me and humiliate me, I want Him to fuck me in every orifice, I imagine His cock moving from my cunt to my ass.

I drink wine and think about blood, my blood, He might like to see it flow, I'm sure my blood forming on my white skin would give Him a hard-on, I can already see the bright gleam in His gray eyes, His thick white sperm flowing in the crimson stripes He'll have adorned my body with.

I want Him so much I could die. I don't understand why He doesn't fuck me. I don't understand the effect He has on me. I don't understand. I'm afraid. I'm afraid of not being worthy of Him. I'm afraid He'll tire of me. I'm afraid He'll want to play other games with another woman. I'd like to make myself indispensable to Him.

My only desire is to be the object of His desire.

I look at the women around me. They've never known the things He's inflicting on me, they've never been paid such a tribute. They haven't been so fortunate. I think again about the women I know who've belonged to Him. Did He treat them the same way? I'll never ask Him, and I'll never know the answer.

My cunt hurts, it's burning for Him.

I'm soaking wet.

I look at my husband and his indifference reassures me. I love him. I care about him, he's my father, my brother, my best friend. I need the family cocoon I've created. I think about my baby.

I'm diving into a bottomless well, but I delight in what I'm feeling. I'm alive.

◆ ◆ ◆

He's pushing His chair back and standing up, and I'm brought back with a jolt to the quai de Béthune.

He's leaving!

My whole body strains in His direction.

I wait for Him to lean over and say good-bye to me, I wait for His lips on my cheek, His hand on my shoulder, a nod of the head, an understanding look.

But He doesn't even turn to look at me.

I hear Him apologize for leaving so soon, He has a case to plead in Orléans or Chartres tomorrow, His taxi's waiting, He's already kissing the hostess and crossing the room to the door, leaving me alone with my inflamed cunt.

Will He even think of the whip?

Will He even remember our date tomorrow?

I hear the door close. I'm alone in the middle of everyone.

I'm carrying the cross of my tortured body, enjoying my suffering in expectation of the pleasure He might derive from it. I remember a sentence by Montherlant—"I think that what I love in her is the pain I cause her"—and for a fleeting moment, I close my eyes and dream that He, too, loves the pain He's inflicting on me.

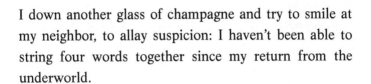

I down another glass of champagne and try to smile at my neighbor, to allay suspicion: I haven't been able to string four words together since my return from the underworld.

My husband takes my arm.

Like a broken doll, I stand up and follow him. All I can think about is the whip hidden in the stroller.

Did He see it and take it?

My husband scolds me gently for drinking too much, or smoking too much, both I suppose. I'm shaky on my feet, and he holds my arm to support me and pulls me out of the apartment.

As we cross the entrance hall, past the child's stroller, his broad body blocks my view, so I'm not able to check whether or not He took the whip.

A few seconds later, I find myself in the car taking me back to the family home. My eyes fill with tears.

What if He didn't find it?

◆ ◆ ◆

As soon as we're home, I rush to the bathroom and lock myself in to relieve my body of the thing that's causing me so much pain.

From the lips of my swollen cunt, I pull a clothespin.

A few hours later, I'm still lying awake with my eyes open in the big bed. My husband's fast asleep.

But I can't get to sleep.

All I can think about is Him. I toss and turn, remembering every minute of the unreal evening. The night is endless.

The next day is worse. He doesn't call me, which means I won't see Him tonight as we arranged.

V

All I can think about is the whip.

I'm convinced He took it. But why doesn't He contact me?

Has He hidden it at home?

Could He—horror of horrors!—have used it on the gorgeous Helen? What kind of relationship do they have?

Does He tell her about me, about us, how He ties me up, how He stuck that ridiculous clothespin on me, how I licked His thumb when He took it out of my ass, how I get wet when He talks to me and refuses to fuck me?

Do they laugh together about His exploits, my dependence, my submissiveness?

All these questions torture me. I cry as my baby and I are

playing with toy cars and he follows the line of my tears with his little angel fingers.

His love and his *Mama*s are what's keeping me alive.

All I can think about is the whip.

I don't understand myself anymore, I scare myself.

How did I come to this?

I remember every one of His words, every one of His gestures, the mark of His fingers on my skin.

The bruise left on my cunt by the clothespin is fading with every day that passes, but when I touch it with my forefinger or my panties rub against it, I still get a slightly painful tingling sensation, which excites me and brings the memory of Him back to me.

I concentrate on the pain as it wears off, but at the same time I can feel a kind of ball, growing in my rib cage as the hours and days go by and I have no news and can't call Him, because I know He wouldn't like it, though I'd really like to be able to say to Him: "Please send for me, I need you to practice your perversions on me, I dream about the touch of the whip on my skin, the whip I gave you, you must make me suffer a little more before you plunge me back into the formaldehyde of nonexistence, because when you let me breathe, when you loosen the rope you use to tie me up, it feels as if I'm sinking inch by inch into a crevasse where you'll leave me to die of cold, and, as it happens, I've always hated the cold, you're my sun, you're my light, without you my senses are numb, nobody has ever treated me like you, nobody will ever treat me like you, I know that, maybe you find this hard to believe but, until now, I've always been a woman men desired, they're always chatting me up or sending me e-mails or flowers, hoping for a date, maybe a kiss, and then you came along! They all think I'm so strong and independent, none of them could ever have imagined being able to make me subservient. Did you realize that? None of them could ever have imagined me now, waiting for you to send for me, to treat me roughly, give me orders, bring me to heel, please teach me a little more, I've lost weight for you, I'm making myself beautiful for you, just you and nobody else, all I want is for you to mistreat me again, just once, you're my Master, you're my God, please don't abandon me like an old woman in an old people's home, I can make you come, I want to feel you coming, no matter where, no matter how, give me the opportunity, you haven't even fucked me, I haven't made your sperm flow, I want to feel it, I want to see it, I want to drink it, drink you to the dregs, I've never even touched your body, never even seen your skin, I want to feel your cock get hard for me, feel it all over with my tongue, I want to feel it deep inside my cunt, or deep inside my ass, it doesn't matter, what matters is you, your desire, your pleasure, I can be good to you, if you give me the chance, I need you to sully me again, I need you to fuck me, I didn't know I was like this, you've revealed me to myself, nobody has ever treated me like you, I'd never played these games before, never even imagined them, now I'm begging you, please keep me awhile longer."

Maybe one day I'll write all that to Him.

For the moment, I keep waiting for His number to flash up. As soon as I enter a meeting, I switch all calls to my secretary's line, as soon as I arrive in the morning I rush to look at the list of calls received by the switchboard in case he rang last night or early this morning. Nothing.

My life is reduced to waiting and Ambien.

I don't eat, I don't work, I don't sleep, I drink green tea and chain-smoke. Gainsbourg was a Gitanes smoker. He's like a cloud that dissolves, a dream, an illusion, a fantasy. I thought I could reach Him, thought I could make Him love me, thought I could make Him need me just a little. But He doesn't care about me at all, He revels in his own indifference.

I look at my girlfriends. I can't talk to them, they wouldn't understand, they couldn't. They tell me all their secrets, that's how I know nobody has ever treated them the way

He treats me. They've never felt this desire, this pleasure of belonging, giving yourself, submitting to a man, just because it's HIM, there's no rational explanation for it, it's like a demonic spell you can't struggle against.

But what has He done with the whip?

During my sleepless nights, I imagine Him using it on other women. I dream about Helen's back arching as He whips her. I dream about Him fucking her, brutally, her cries, her orgasm, Him drying her tears with His kisses.

What has He done to reduce me to this state? Is it just the fact that He's resisting me or has He put a spell on me? Is it something else? I hardly know Him. But all I want is to see Him again.

My girlfriends regularly see psychics. Nice, kind ladies who predict the future for them, a future that's not too rosy but not too gray.

I have lunch with my friend Claire, who's also a lawyer and has a little girl not much younger than my son. While we're having coffee, one of her favorite psychics comes and joins her. Maybe when they leave they're planning to burn a little holy grass, or spread some salt around her apartment, or swing a pendulum.

I'm surprised by the woman.

She doesn't know a thing about me, but as soon as she sits down, she says: "You're having a steamy affair with a man who's put a spell on you. He's treating you as nobody will ever treat you."

I beg her to see me as soon as she can.

The woman's really amazing. She's a concierge and sees me in her lodge, and the first thing she talks about is her cellar, which is flooded. True, it's been raining nonstop for days, you don't have to be a psychic to notice that. The water's reached the foundations of the building, and the owners are in a quandary because they don't have any decent boots to wear and can't come and estimate the damage, so she equipped herself with a little bucket and set off to confront the liquid that's seeping into the walls. She keeps talking about herself and the water while I'm longing to hear about me and Him.

At last, sensing my impatience, she looks me in the eyes and repeats the same words: "You're having a steamy affair with a man who's put a spell on you. He's treating you as nobody will ever treat you."

I urge her to continue.

She asks me if I have any letters, photos, a garment belonging to Him.

I take out a little photo of Him I found in *L'Express.*

She shudders.

"I see a woman with a hood. Your friend has very particular sexual tastes. He's ambitious. At the moment, he's living with a blond woman, who's tall and thin and very beautiful. He also has you, plus another woman, a brunette, who's very young."

She stops, closes her eyes, resumes: "You won't have an easy time. You're going to suffer. You feel as if you're possessed. You're going to experience a real passion. He's always around. He'll send for you more and more often. It'll go on for a long time, several months at least. He'll demand to see you all the time. You'll have a difficult summer. You'll suffer. He'll make you do incredible things, but you'll ask for more. Be careful."

I smile at her in gratitude. This was more than I expected. "He wants to see you all the time." Her words echo in my head.

"But will He ever think highly of me? Will I ever matter to Him? Even a little?"

For a few minutes she's silent, with her eyes closed, and her head pressed between her hands. She resumes: "He has no feelings for you. At best, take him as a ray of sunshine that warms your body and your heart before it's hidden again by the clouds."

Her words sting me but I insist.

"When will I hear from Him?"

She suggests a second deck of cards.

I cut the cards with my left hand and, with the same hand, give her fifteen cards.

Conscientiously, she spreads them out in two columns around the one representing me.

One by one, the figures are revealed. I don't know anything about it but I try to guess their symbolism.

She goes on without looking at me: "You must be careful. You're going to hear from him. But this man is really very unhealthy. He's making you ill."

She shows me a card depicting a woman lying on a bed, suffering, then another showing a man lying down, draped with a sheet.

"This is him. All he thinks about is sex. But he has

money and power, too. He lives with someone, quite happily. Does he live with someone?"

I nod, thinking of "His" Helen.

"You haven't answered the only question that matters to me. When will I hear from Him? When will I see Him again?"

"If you only have one question, I can do a Marseille tarot for you. But I must warn you: I don't do it very often. It's horrible. It tells the truth. It knows. You might be disappointed."

"I'll take the risk. I want to know. Please. I'm not afraid."

"If you insist. You must really concentrate on your question. Keep thinking of it and take out the cards."

She takes another deck from her drawer.

I have only one thought in my head: Will He call me? Will He see me again?

Still with my left hand, I give her ten cards, one after the other, and she turns them over as I give them to her, around the card she's chosen to represent me.

The figures are different from the Persian tarot. Some seem very figurative, others more esoteric.

"This is you," she says. "You'll hear from him. He'll make you a proposition. You'll have to come to a decision.

You're being given a choice. On one side, you can have everything. This card is called the World, it means opportunity, success, victory. On the other . . ."

She pauses, seems to hesitate. "Are you sure you want to know everything?"

I nod.

"On the other," she resumes, showing me a card representing the Devil, "on the other, there's hell, sex, lust. Cover this card."

I hand her a card. She turns it over. A sort of tower, the top of it broken and falling.

"This is the Tower, which means decline. A lot of suffering."

Her voice grows harder.

"This man is extremely unhealthy. He enjoys the suffering he inflicts on you. He's extremely perverted. He'll make you his slave. He'll take complete control of you and bring about your downfall. He'll mistreat you. You'll suffer. He'll torture you. There's no point in going on. I wouldn't want you to draw the worst."

I laugh. Nervousness, I suppose.

"Please, let me. I'll choose success, you'll see. I'll win."

I take a card from the covered pack and hand it to her.

She places her hand over mine. "Are you sure?"

I smile. "It can't be any worse," I insist, convinced I'm right.

But I'm wrong.

As she turns over the card, I see her go white and take her head in her hands again. She doesn't say anything.

I lean over the card to try to understand. I see the image of a woman wrapped in a cape or a long coat that covers her from head to foot. In her raised hand, she's brandishing a large knife.

"You shouldn't have. I told you."

"Tell me. I prefer to hear. Am I going to die?"

The seconds pass. They seem endless.

"No. Death is only drawn as a 'cover.' This isn't a physical death, not a murder, anyway. But listen, you must be careful. I've never drawn a pack like this. The Devil, then the Tower, then Death. This man is terrible. He can destroy you completely, sweep away everything you've built up. Your marriage, your family, your work. Everything can explode. You must take care of yourself, my dear. You're an intelligent, sensible woman; you have a family, a husband who loves you, a child who needs you. Don't see him again. Please, I know it's a great temptation, but think about what I'm saying, don't see him again.

"You're going to ruin your life. He really isn't worth it. He represents everything that's most terrible. There's nothing in the relationship except sex and lust. It takes

you over completely, makes you ill. He enslaves you.
Despises you. Destroys you morally and physically. The
more he harms you, the more pleasure he feels.

"One day, a woman will get killed. Really."

Another long pause.

"I can't go on. I'm shivering. Touch my hands!"

I take her hands. They're ice-cold. I shiver, too.

"I beg you," she insists. "Your fate isn't sealed. It
depends on the decision you make. Don't see him again.
You'll lose everything."

She points to the last of the cards that are spread out in
front of her, and tells me it represents the Pilgrim and His
Staff.

"Look, your whole life will be destroyed. Think of the
people you really love, the people around you. Don't
destroy everything. Not for that! He isn't worth it. He
doesn't deserve you. You're too young, too fresh. I
beseech you, take care of your life."

Stunned, I pay her and leave. I walk along the street without even knowing where I am. The woman didn't know
me, but she seemed so sincere, so close to me, so sure of
herself. I'm shaken. *He has no feelings for you. All he
thinks about is sex. One day, a woman will get killed.* Her
words sear my soul.

◆ ◆ ◆

If He sends for me, I'll go. I know it.

I'm not capable of resisting Him.

At the same time, I care so much about my life, I don't want to destroy anything, I certainly don't want to hurt anybody.

But I also NEED to see Him again. The things He's given me the chance to experience are too strong. I just can't resist the way my heart starts racing as soon as I think of Him. He was right, it's just as He predicted: I can no longer have an orgasm without thinking about Him, my whole life is permeated with Him; I've become His thing, His slave, deprived of judgment, I'm well and truly under a spell.

The woman is right. He's the Devil and He's made me His subject, without my being aware of it, and now I'm incapable of resisting Him, incapable of escaping Him. I'm His as Mary is God's. Lord, protect me, what's to become of me?

I'm already waiting for another call, already looking for a way to see Him again, to remind Him of my existence. But if that woman is to be believed, I ought to give up any hope of Him ever having any real affection for me.

That night, I close my eyes and wonder why, and how, I got to this point, I who had everything.

VI

The "file" I've put together about Him tells me His birthday is May 13. After hesitating for a long time between a black tie, white orchids, and a pair of handcuffs, I opt for a Lalique statuette of a woman, in a prostrate, almost huddled position. I recognize in it all the suffering of a woman dependent on the desire of the Master to whom she has given herself.

The statuette is perfectly smooth and perfectly round, and the sanded crystal has a sensuous feel, at once sophisticated and primitive. Its symbolism is clear.

When the day comes, I have it sent to His office.

◆ ◆ ◆

He doesn't call me.

One day, He'll tell me He doesn't want it on His desk, it has no place in His life. I'll receive this strange thank-you like a bird, a bullet in flight.

He'll see fit to add: "You know, dear Élodie, it's good to be disappointed by one's friends, that way nobody has any illusions."

I'll never know what became of the statuette.

Sometimes, I think about that crystal woman kneeling submissively. I wonder where she is, if she survived to be cherished and caressed by other hands, or if she's half dead half alive in her gray coffin, waiting for a tender look to wake her one day.

VII

I run into my handsome friend Hassan at the Palais de Justice. He's in such a bad mood, it breaks my heart.

Since he started defending the man who killed all those crippled old ladies in that chain of old people's homes, the press has been taking endless potshots at him, and he's worn out. His client's stubborn denials, despite all the evidence against him, have gotten them both into a morass, and he's running out of ideas for how to get them out of it.

All the same, he seems happy to see me and eager to talk. He suggests we meet in the place Dauphine.

◆ ◆ ◆

So I sit down in the Bar du Caveau and wait. Time passes. When he doesn't come, I quickly dial his cell-phone number.

"Hello, where are you? I'm waiting for you in the Bar du Caveau. What's up?"

There's a jumble of noise.

"Can you hear me? It's Élodie. Can you hear me? Hello?"

I can't hear anything, except some unpleasant crackling. "Hassan?" I repeat stubbornly. "Hassan, can you hear me?"

"Who do you want to talk to?"

"Hassan? Hassan, is that you?"

"No, Élodie. It isn't Hassan, it's your subconscious!"

All at once, I recognize His voice and become all flustered.

"I'm sorry," I stammer. "I'm sorry, I didn't mean to disturb you, really, I didn't mean to call you, I dialed the wrong number."

But He's already hung up, and I see Hassan coming toward me with that supple walk of his, like a real man of the desert.

◆ ◆ ◆

When he sees the blush on my cheeks, he bursts out laughing.

I want to cry.

I no longer know where I am. It's as if I'm living in a bubble, cut off from everyone and everything. I find it hard to concentrate on my briefs. I performed miserably in my last riding competition. All I think about is Him, I belong to Him and nobody else. A few months ago, I was thinking about having another child. Now I can't even make love to my husband. Fortunately, he's away so often on business, he doesn't seem to notice. Sometimes, I tell myself he must have mistresses who compensate for the disastrous sex life I give him. Not that I really care. And yet, deep down, I know he's still the bedrock of my life, the meaning of my existence. I don't want to leave him, the thought of hurting him is more than I can bear, but I have no misgivings, I don't even feel as if I'm cheating on him. Because He isn't a lover, He isn't my lover, it's not about feelings, not even about sex, He hardly even touches me, certainly doesn't fuck me. It's an unreal, abstract relationship, and I don't know what it means. Sometimes I tell myself it's only a fantasy, He's only a fantasy, a mental construct invented by a young woman who's had everything she needs out of life and now wants to experience something stronger, and yet at the same time I'm certain He's changed my life, that He really does hold sway over me and is gradually poisoning me like a dangerous drug I can't break free of. The psychic was right, He must have cast a spell on me.

VIII

It's over.

He's telling me He's lost His desire for me.

After all this waiting and hoping and dreaming of His hands on me, He phones to invite me, in a voice as polite as it's kind, to accompany Him to an awards ceremony, where adventurous young lawyers receive recognition for their oratory.

I'm at the end of the phone, unable to breathe. My heart stops beating. I understand.

I stumble a bit, stammer a kind of "Why not?" I try to hide my dismay, regain my composure, tell Him I'm very pleased. At least He's sufficiently well bred to show me I'm more than just a doll you can blindfold and torture with clothespins.

Anyway, when I think about it, I realize it's better to see Him again, even like this, even if it's always going to be like this. For the first time, He's showing me some consideration, He's going to take me out in public, the whole of the bar association will be there and I'll be at His side.

His words echo deep down in my heart, convincing me to accept: "There's nothing wrong with two friends going to a professional engagement together."

Two friends, two friends.

Can we really be friends? I've suffered so much, wanted His body so much, wanted at last to feel His cock inside me, just once, His unknown cock, needed Him to take out just a little of His perverted frenzy on me again.

His secretary calls mine to ask me to pick Him up at his office.

So be it.

I feel completely disoriented.

I think of wearing jeans and sandals, just to show Him that I expect nothing more of Him, that I've understood, and to spare myself the final humiliation of getting all prepared to be His object and finding He doesn't even deign to make use of me.

I'm supposed to be having lunch with a girlfriend, but she cancels, giving me a chance to spend some time with my beloved mare. I'm happy to see her again, I stroke her shiny mane and kiss the star adorning her nose and hug her neck and whisper in her ear that I really need her because I'm a bit sad and only she can cheer me up.

Later, galloping along the sandy avenues of the Bois de Boulogne, I feel her heart between my legs, her powerful muscles as she gallops, carrying me along with her. We form one body; I think about nothing except this beloved horse I know so well, who shakes her head when she sees me. I stroke her rounded neck and forget everything, think about nothing, I'm just fine.

She's sweating, her veins stand out. Whenever we come to a dangerous road, she stamps the ground before crossing.

By the time I dismount, I'm exhausted, drained but happy, my neck and temples bathed in sweat, ready to face His indifference with all the self-confidence I can muster.

———◆———

That mad gallop has given me the calm and balance I needed.

When evening comes, I stand in the shower for a long time, eyes closed, and let the water flow over my shoulders. I know He knows I'm coming and how impatient I am to see Him again. I'm quite determined to remain totally in control of myself. I don't put on any makeup, put my hair up in a bun, and run a Chinese pin through it and put on a little black-and-white cotton dress, buttoned all the way down. But, as a matter of form, I also put on high, black, open sandals.

I arrive outside His office, and call up to suggest He come down, which will avoid me having to park. At least He'll know I've understood.

"I'm on the phone. I won't be long. Park your car and come up. I still have a couple of little things to see to."

His assistant opens the door for me. I recognize her, a young auburn-haired woman with long, slim legs and a high rump. I met her when we were both looking at files in the legal records office.

I wonder how He treats her. At her invitation, I sit down in the waiting room like a good girl and listen for the sound of His steps. All at once, I feel a little less determined. I become aware that my heart is beating faster.

I haven't seen Him for two months. When He appears I hold my breath.

He's wearing a light suit and tie.

I've never seen Him in anything but a black suit before. With a black tie.

He smiles, holds out His hand, and kisses me on the cheek.

I'm prepared. I pretend to be relaxed and really pleased at the prospect of going out with Him.

But He takes a few steps back and looks me up and down. Gradually, His expression changes. I recognize that look in His eyes, I've dreamed about it.

"Of course," is all He says.

I know my dress fits me like a glove, I know I'm a lot slimmer now, I've noticed the looks I've been getting from men in the street.

My high black sandals have four very thin straps that cross over my foot, like ropes tying a body.

His eyes linger on them.

He likes me. He quickly draws me to Him and touches my skin.

Without even a word from Him, I join my hands behind my back.

He smiles. He knows I haven't forgotten.

"I thought you didn't like me anymore," I say, in a whisper.
  "You were wrong."

I want to ask Him why, why so long? But I don't dare. Of course.
  "What time do we have to leave? Where is it?"
  "We have time."

His hands have climbed up my bare thighs.
  His hands undo the buttons of my dress.
  His hands take hold of my breasts and pull them out of my bra.
  Without Him asking, I arch my back.
  He strokes my buttocks and slaps them with the flat of His hand.

He asks me if I've missed His blows.
  I don't reply, just lower my head. That wasn't me—He's never hit me. I know it's not a deliberate mistake. I don't say a word. I don't have time to feel sad, or the right to be jealous.

Still smiling at me, He strokes the back of my neck with His fingers, then asks me to touch Him.

◆

For the first time, He's there in front of me and I'm not blindfolded.

Without removing His trousers, he takes His cock out. I'm fascinated by it, it's so broad and heavy, and so taut it looks as if it's about to explode. I'd like to take it in my hand, but He pushes my hand away and grabs a handful of my hair and pulls my head down until my mouth is on His engorged cock. I try to swallow it, but find it hard to get my lips round it, my throat catches. I suck it very slowly between my closed lips, really applying myself, lingering on the tip. My tongue comes and goes, licking, lingering on the most sensitive spots. I concentrate on His pleasure, which I can feel rising. I take it deep in my throat again, then pull it out again very slowly, accentuating the pressure of my lips, aware that His breathing is getting faster. I take my time. I stop when I feel His pleasure mounting and for a few seconds I slow it down, keeping only the end of His cock on my tongue, before plunging it deep in my throat again, savoring with infinite slowness every fraction of an inch of His most precious, most fragile asset.

◆ ◆ ◆

I feel His left hand slip between my thighs. He introduces one finger into my anus, then two. I think it's just two. He pushes His fingers all the way in. He seems to be creating a loop deep inside me, with a slow and sustained rhythm, the same rhythm with which I'm sucking Him. I want Him.

I NEED HIS COCK INSIDE ME.

But although I haven't yet made Him come, He's already walking away.

"I'm going to put a little dildo inside you for the evening. It'll be fun, you'll see. Don't move."

He goes and rummages in one of His desk drawers.

I don't dare move an inch. He's placed one of my legs on a chair, so that my back is even more arched. My breasts are out of my bra. I wait, not daring to turn around and look at Him. But He's already behind me.

I haven't seen the thing. He kneels in front of me, opens my cunt, and plunges an oblong rubber object into it.

I have to hold back a shudder.

He smiles and moves forward on my right.

"Touch yourself. Quicker."

I obey.

"Wait."

I stop. In His hand is a kind of pearl rosary.

He lightly touches my breasts, which strain toward Him.

There are little slipknots at both ends of the rosary. He ties them round my nipples, very light, like a garrote. My nipples turn blue.

"Does it hurt?"
   "Yes."
   "Do you like it?"
   "I don't know."
   "You have to get used to the pain. Touch yourself again."

I overcome my usual modesty and obey. Luckily, part of my dress has fallen, which means He can't see this very intimate thing I'm doing, can't see me touching my cunt with my fingers.

He's taken a step back, and He's looking at me and smiling.
   He's touching himself, too.
   I'm overcome with emotion. I haven't seen Him for two months and I've forgotten how good it was.
   "Touch yourself. Don't stop. That's it."
   His voice is urgent, commanding, just like my dreams.
   I concentrate.

"Come. Now. I want to hear you cry out."

As if my senses are connected to His, the orgasm immediately contorts my body. I bite my hand to hold back my cries.

"You're beautiful. Let's go now."

"I'm not going to the conference wearing these things, am I?"

"Of course you are! What do you take me for? I forbid you to touch them!"

I don't dare protest, and I follow Him outside without another word.

The people in the street stare at me. I'm sure they're puzzled by the hesitant way I'm walking.

I look at the women and wonder if any of them can guess that between each unsteady step I feel a sharp pain in the three strategic points of my body.

I tell myself that none of them has ever received such a tribute.

I'm proud of Him.

I'm proud to be His.

I get painfully into my car and try to concentrate on my driving, without much success.

He tells me off for not taking the shortest route.

Before I can stop myself, I reply that I'm not used to driving with this thing stuck inside me, and then immediately apologize for my insolence.

He smiles and orders me to get over it.

◆ ◆ ◆

As if all the gods have conspired against me, the parking lot in the place Dauphine is full.

"Just drop me here, we'll meet inside." And He quickly gets out of the car, leaving me to park it. I'm a bit upset by His rudeness, but don't dare say anything. I think of my husband, and how much he respects me.

Naturally, there's no parking space nearby, and I have to walk two hundred yards to join Him.

The whole of the Paris Bar is here. He ignores me, or pretends to. I realize He doesn't want us to be seen together.

I move through the gathering—as much as I can with this thing tearing me apart—and a few minutes later find myself in the hall, sitting next to a colleague I don't know.

As for Him, He's sat down next to a former president of the Bar Association and is showing off. After all, He's a leading light of the Bar and it means a lot to Him.

The speeches start. All I can think about is Him and the object cutting my body in two.

My neighbor must be wondering about my state of health, he keeps looking at me anxiously as I change position to try to lessen the pain.

On the other hand, my breasts have almost stopped hurting. I must have gotten used to it.

When the speeches stop, a former "first secretary" comes up and kisses me and invites me to the cocktail party he's giving after the conference, in the big waiting hall. I thank him, pretty sure I'll be able to get out of it, and sit down again carefully on my chair.

But by now His neighbor's left the hall and He signals for me to join Him. I do as he asks, threading my way with difficulty through my colleagues. I see the handsome Hassan and kiss him. Hassan watches me with what seems to me a mocking smile as I go to Him.

At last I reach Him and sit down next to Him. The current president of the Bar Association starts speaking.

"Have you any idea what you're making me do?"

"Of course."

I'm happy.

The pain is unbearable.

My body feels bloated, I try to find a position that will make me less aware of the size of the object inside me, but each time I move, my insides seem to swell even more, screaming in protest.

I see Him smile, and while everyone's hanging on the words of a man who represents law and order, He puts His hand under my buttocks and pushes the object even farther in.

He slides His hands under my dress and puts His fingers inside my panties.

He rubs my cunt and immediately lifts His fingers to my mouth.

"Wipe my fingers. You're soaking wet."

I'm more excited than I've ever been in my life.

The president of the Bar Association makes a moving speech about a colleague of ours whose talent for oratory was recognized by everyone and who died recently at the age of forty-two, struck down by a sudden cancer. He was my best friend. In fact, he was almost like a big brother. We went to parties together, shared many carefree times. I remember going to see him at his parents' little house in the place des Vosges, knowing I'd probably never see him again, I remember hugging him, I remember his face when he looked at me for the last time.

Suddenly He takes my hand.

I could die right now and not regret a thing.

I stroke His fingers, massage His palm, squeeze His thumb—which I'd really love to put in my mouth—and follow the lines on His hand with my nails.

It's the first tender gesture He's ever shown toward me. The emotion I feel is stronger than the pain of the dildo.

—◆—

Everyone stands. I beg Him to spare me the Bar Association cocktail party.

I'm unsteady on my legs. I feel as if I'm wide open.

No, He whispers in my ear, He's expecting me to go to the party and show I'm worthy of Him. To overcome any attempt at resistance, He places an imperious hand on my hip.

I don't dare answer.

Everyone is here. I see Hassan again. He introduces me to his Victoria, who looks like she's come straight from the Ford Model Agency. She doesn't touch the petits fours, the sight of Hassan is all the food she needs. The whole of the Bar Association council is here, and all the new secretaries surrounded by their adoring parents, smiling and exchanging polite chitchat.

I accept the glass of champagne I'm handed. The alcohol will make me feel more at ease.

I hope with all my heart that He loves what He's making me do. Discussing the merits of judges in financial cases with my buttocks pulled apart by a dildo is no easy task. I'm drunk on champagne and weak with hunger. For a moment, the whole thing comes home to me: here I am, at this ritzy party, full of members of the Bar, which is my

world, the world where I'm trying to carve out a niche for
myself, with a dildo stuck inside me and my nipples
imprisoned by knots. I rise to my full height and smile,
trying to seem as natural as possible.

I'm pleased to see my good friend Sara. She's as dark as
I'm blond, as high-spirited as I'm introverted. I hug her
and kiss her affectionately. I'd like to be able to tell her,
but I know nobody would understand.

He's been talking to a young woman, making her laugh.
Now I see Him move away from her and come toward us.
He whispers in my ear that He's proud of me. I feel ready for
anything. Then, with total nonchalance, He turns to Sara
and asks her if she's noticed anything unusual about me.

Sara is clever enough, and close enough to me, to know
He's not talking about business law anymore. She laughs
gaily and says I'm quite secretive. Then she looks closely
at me and says no, but she does think I'm looking very
slim and very beautiful. I thank her with a look, trying not
to let her see how flustered I am.

"Look closer."
    Sara puts out her hand, touches my chest lightly, and
moves over my stomach.

"She's lost a lot of weight."

"That doesn't matter. Concentrate."

However hard she stares at me, she can't see anything.

"Turn around," he says to me.

I immediately turn.

"Look at your friend, Sara. She's completely submissive. She's capable of great things. Compared with her, you're a child."

I blush at the compliment.

"Touch her."

Sara touches my shoulders, moves her hand down my back.

My back is naturally very arched, but now it's even more so.

In the middle of this big hall, with our most brilliant colleagues gathered around us, Sara stops at the small of my back.

"Is she wearing a bustier?"

I laugh and shake my head.

"She's wearing a G-string."

"Not just that."

"I really don't understand."

"Go on. Keep touching her. All over."

Although Sara and I are quite intimate, and she tells me all about her love life, I've never dared talk to her about

my enslavement, and I feel very embarrassed at the
thought that she might find out about it like this.

I feel her hand moving over my buttocks and hips and I
tremble. I feel sure she's going to discover the foreign
body inside me.

"Come on, now, don't you know your friend's body?"

Puzzled, she moves back up toward my chest and holds
back a cry of surprise as she touches one of my nipples,
which is squeezed tight by the garrote and makes a bump
the size of a big walnut under my thin dress.

"What's this? What have you done to her?"

"Guess," He whispers in her ear. "Imagine those
breasts in your mouth."

She immediately blushes. All of a sudden, she seems
disconcerted. He smiles and kisses the back of my neck.
I'm very grateful to Him for not forcing my friend to
explore any further.

"Come on. It's time."

I follow Him like a blind woman, and pray with all my
might that none of the assembled guests has noticed how
strangely I'm behaving.

When we reach my car, I don't feel capable of driving and
I ask Him to take the wheel.

He acquiesces with a smile, and I sit down awkwardly beside Him. The pain is intense. I feel as if I'm being torn in pieces.

"Where are we going?"

"You must learn to keep quiet. There are some questions I haven't given you permission to ask."

I don't say any more, just let Him drive.

We reach the avenue de l'Opéra. He turns from the avenue onto the rue Thérèse and parks at the end.

I open the door to get out.

"You can take it out now."

"Here?"

I lift myself up in the car and put my left hand under my dress.

I can feel the rubbery base of the object. I slowly extricate it from deep inside me.

No sooner have I taken it out than He slips two fingers between my bruised buttocks.

"That's perfect, you're well spread now."

He moves his fingers to the front.

"You're soaking. You're drenched."

He's right. I want Him.

We walk along the street and He takes me by the hand. I'll never get used to His occasional shows of affection. The touch of His hand excites me and I want to kiss

Him but He doesn't kiss me.

We stop in front of a black door, under a sign showing nothing but a bull's-eye. He pulls me to Him and
hugs me.

"Listen to me. You're mine. You'll stay mine. Even if
other men touch you, even if I order you to touch other
men's cocks, or women, I'm your Master and I want to be
proud of you."

"You have nothing to be afraid of."

"I'm here. I'll protect you."

He pushes open the big black door.

We find ourselves in a little foyer, with a closed door at
the end. He rings. A few seconds later, the door is opened
by a woman in a severe black suit.

We enter a kind of cloakroom.

I hand Him my jacket and my handbag.

He takes me by the shoulders and pulls me toward a
small spiral staircase.

At the bottom of the steps there is a buffet of sugary
petits fours and Haribo candies.

Then a nightclub of the most classic kind, with a bar and
a bartender and a little dance floor on which people are
shimmying, hardly more high-spirited or more undressed
than they would be at a club like the Queen.

◆ ◆ ◆

He hands me a glass of champagne—the umpteenth of the evening—and sits down on a stool beside me and puts His arm around my shoulders. I turn toward Him and kiss Him as hard as I can. He returns my kiss, with surprising tenderness. I'm completely carried away.

The room is dark, much darker than in a "normal" club.

I look around me at the people: a lot of young women, some of them quite pretty. I don't look at the men.

I feel I'm His.

The atmosphere of male lust is palpable, and it makes me uncomfortable. I search for His hand and squeeze it. His arm is still around me, protecting me from any approach by third parties. But just as I'm starting to relax, He stands up and pulls me after Him.

He pushes me into a corridor to the left of the dance floor.

I hold my breath and listen. I'm startled to hear moans of pleasure and heavy breathing coming from an almost dark room.

After a few seconds, my eyes adjust to the darkness and I make out a wide bench seat where a woman is kneeling, sucking a man's cock, almost oblivious to the fact that two other men have their hands on her cunt and are fondling it, sometimes taking turns, sometimes together.

To their right, a man is lying on his back and two girls are masturbating him. Their hands crisscross as they climb up and down his cock.

Some distance away, a woman is being fucked doggy style—and making a lot of noise about it.

On the wall to the left, there's a kind of cross with a man tied to it. He's on his own, apparently abandoned. I notice he has a huge hard-on.

I jump. Someone's touching me and it's not Him.

I haven't let go of His hand, and now I squeeze it with all my might. He pushes the pest away.

He takes me by the shoulders and pushes me in front of him along the corridor. On the right is an alcove hollowed out of a cobbled wall. He pulls back the curtain.

Two couples are lying there, languidly.

The two men are rather potbellied, and one of the women, who's very thin, seems at least as old as my mother. I'm struck by the sad expression on her face.

I catch myself hoping I won't be here, making a spectacle of myself, in thirty years' time.

We continue along the corridor and come to a large square room. The whole right-hand side is covered with a huge bed.

At the far end of the room there's a recess behind a wire mesh door.

It's quite dark here and I can't see very well, but it looks like a cage.

On the big mattress, a few naked bodies, entwined. In front of them, several couples, embracing, fondling.

The room is surprisingly silent.

He's placed Himself behind me, with His arms around my shoulders. He brushes my cheek and the back of my neck with His lips.

I close my eyes. I'm happy.

I'm in a swingers' club with a man who treats me as if I were nothing, who doesn't show me the slightest affection, the slightest feeling, who lives with another girl, and plays around with several others, a man who hasn't called me for two months then takes me to a meeting of our colleagues with a dildo inside me, tearing me apart, but I'm fine. I feel more fulfilled right now than I've been for a very long time, fulfilled by the smallest sign of tenderness from Him.

But now He takes His arms away from me and takes my hand and pulls me out again into the corridor, which leads to other back rooms.

There's only one couple left in the first room we passed.

A very white man whose face I can't make out has his

mouth in the cunt of a young woman with long slender legs.

She's on her back, her legs wide open, arching her upper body, biting her fingers and throwing her head back.

She's slim, with small breasts that point upward.

He squeezes my hand and for a few minutes we stand there watching them. We don't speak, just watch this beautiful young woman, her face contorted as her pleasure mounts.

"Go ahead," He whispers in my ear.

I tremble and try to look in His eyes. But He's staring at the girl.

He lets go of my hand.

"Go on, now. Take her."

Overcoming my shyness, I walk unsteadily toward the couple. There's a knot in my stomach, but I really don't want to let Him down.

Slowly, shaking with trepidation, I sit down beside them, then edge forward on the bed. I'm frozen with nervousness, but try to overcome it and reach out my hand toward her breasts. I'm afraid she'll push me away, but she seizes my hand in hers and places it on one of her breasts.

The room is very dark, but I can feel the softness of her skin and the hardness of her nipple.

I stroke her breast and follow the outline of her nipple with the tip of my finger.

I turn to look at Him.

He's smiling at me. Encouraged by this, I feel confident enough to go further, and for the first time I touch and then hug a woman's body that isn't mine.

He sits down behind me, and I let Him stroke my hair and my buttocks and my cunt.

The girl sits up and draws my face to hers.

She kisses me.

I feel her tongue in my mouth, our bodies merge, her kiss is infinitely sweet, and her skin is silky. I'm discovering a woman's body, and it's incredibly supple and slender.

He's still touching me. He's taken my breasts out of my bra. The garrote is still there, and the nipples are hard and protuberant. The girl's kisses get more intense, and she strokes my breasts.

We touch each other, taste each other's tongues, her jade-black hair merges with my long blond hair, I can feel Him behind me, I can sense how proud He is, my senses are racing.

The young woman's kisses are a little sugary, and so is the back of her neck, I sniff it, breathe it in.

◆ ◆ ◆

Her lover sits up and tries to touch me. He puts his hand on the small of my back and moves it slowly down between my legs.

I look at Him anxiously. He smiles at me and grabs the man's hand. Then He gathers my hair behind my neck and pulls on it, guiding my face between the girl's legs.

I know what He wants me to do. I'm still hesitant, doubtful, but His action gives me strength. He leans toward me and whispers to me to get on with it.

"Do it, now, make her come, I want to see you suck her, do it."

I submit, and for the first time touch a woman's cunt, so brown and hairy and thick, so different, I'm afraid of disappointing Him, disappointing her, not knowing how, I search with my finger, insert it between the labia, gently push it in, she's very wet, whether from the man's saliva or her own juices I don't know, my finger meets something hard, I think I've found it, I part the skin and hair a little and plunge my face and nose and mouth between her slender legs and into her cunt, which is so strange and yet must be like mine, my tongue lingers, turns, accelerates, I concentrate, apply myself, trust to my instinct or my unconscious, I don't know which, my senses are guiding me, I push my tongue in and gently lick, it's slightly bitter, slightly acidic, like a tiny lime on which I'm sucking, turning it in my mouth, I can smell it and the smell excites me, so I venture a little farther, introducing first one finger then two, and massage the interior of her vagina, press on her inner wall as if I wanted to push it aside, press my nose into her cunt, while my other hand grows bolder and goes a little farther down and searches for her anus and I immediately put my middle finger inside, taking care not to hurt her, not to scratch her with my nail, her pelvis strains toward me and I feel as if her womb is opening.

I keep sucking and licking her, moving slowly in and out, I feel the pressure of her mucous membranes on my fingers as I continue burrowing inside her, she stretches, arches, offers herself up. She's shaking, my tongue is determined, resolute, my forefinger works faster, stronger, assisted by my tongue, I can feel her sweat, the moisture of her mounting excitement blinds me like tears, she's dug her fingers into my hair, she clings to it, bracing herself, and suddenly she screams and her orgasm overwhelms her and inflames me.

I've stopped moving my head, my fingers are still deep inside her orifices. I wait. I hear her cry mounting, continuing, becoming more intense, then fading away in a moan, a last spasm.

I sit up and see His face. He kisses me, sucks my tongue, hugs me against Him. His tenderness bewitches me.

I want to feel His hands gliding up my thighs to my buttocks and removing the G-string.

My hands move to His cock. My body is aching for it.

I'm overwhelmed with desire for Him. I beg Him to take me: "Please, take me, fuck me, it doesn't matter how, but do it now, I can't wait any longer, I want it so much, I've dreamed about it so many times, if only You knew, I've dreamed and dreamed, I so much want to be Yours, You've taken possession of me, I'm Yours, I'm Yours, please, fuck me, fuck me, without stopping, I want to make you come, I want to make you come till you cry out. Please, beat my buttocks with your cock, your violence will be incredibly sweet to me, I'll forget the girl next to me and the man who's on his feet now and the circle that's formed around us, and I'll bury my head in the sheet that bears the traces of so much fucking and cry out.

"You'll cry out, too.

"Our fingers will clasp and unclasp, and we'll collapse together."

He squeezes my buttocks and His nails dig into my skin, and His fingers touch my clitoris, and I squeeze His hands in mine, squeeze them like a madwoman, and arch toward

Him, open for Him, but He doesn't fuck me, and I set off on a journey where I'm alone and He's only a dream.

It's three in the morning when I drop Him in front of His building.

"See you very soon," He says, and then He's gone.

I spend the whole night with my eyes open, remembering every minute of that incredible evening.

To live only for that, just once.

The next day, there's a meeting to decide on a tricky legal strategy, which requires all my attention. The phone rings.

I recognize His number and my heart stops beating. I quickly pick up the receiver and press it against my ear so that my colleagues can't hear.

"Remarkable. You were remarkable." And He's already hung up.

IX

I decide to throw a dinner party with my young friend Léa and her legendary Aurélien. When I go to see her to give her back the famous Prada suit she lent me for Léon's dinner, she finally explains why Aurélien, who's over fifty, has such a demonic reputation. For nearly three years now, she tells me with a gleam in her eyes, he's been making her submit to all his desires, even the most outlandish, and they've still not gone as far as they can in their games.

Spontaneously, she opens up to me about his sexual tastes, which she describes as "sophisticated," and proudly shows me the muzzle he's just given her. I even catch a glimpse, in her "magic drawer," of what seem to be a number of "toys" of various sizes and circumferences, together with the kind of ropes I've never seen before except on the decks of sailing boats.

I suspect a dinner for the four of us might be rather interesting. Without going into details about my relationship with Him, I suggest that maybe one day we could all get together with a "friend" of mine who's also a bit "cerebral." Léa claps her hands with joy and promises to put my idea to her beloved Aurélien.

On my side, I tell Him He probably has a lot in common with my beautiful friend and her distinguished comrade. He accepts my plan with a smile, which I interpret as a sign of overwhelming enthusiasm.

Aurélien makes a reservation at the Maison Blanche, which he thinks is fitting for our proposed debauchery.

On the morning of the dinner, He calls me at work and arranges to meet me at Erès, in the place de la Madeleine. He doesn't tell me why.

I'm there at one o'clock on the dot. He's waiting for me in the street.

"I'm going to give you a present."

I look at Him in surprise.

◆ ◆ ◆

In the glass window of the boutique, there are only a few anorexic plastic dummies to attract the attention of passersby to the artistically displayed swimsuits and lingerie. There are several women in the shop, but also a few men fingering the Lycra and tulle garments.

Full of self-confidence, He approaches the cash register and addresses the young saleswoman without the slightest hesitation.

"I'd like Mademoiselle to try on your black tulle bustier—38D."

The young saleswoman hands me a tulle garment, as elegant as it's sober.

"The fitting rooms are at the back of the shop, on the right."

"We also need stockings and a G-string," He says.

I smile, thank her, and walk to the fitting room. He follows close behind me—as I expected He would, to be honest. My cunt is throbbing between my legs as He pulls the curtain shut behind us.

I undress in front of Him, a little embarrassed. I don't think He's ever seen me without the fetishist accessories He likes to use. The mirrors all around the walls reflect every curve of my body. He helps me to do up the hooks on the bustier. I put on the stockings, sliding them up my legs, and step back into my pointed stilettos.

I'm quite pleased with the results of my anorexic diet and turn to Him, smiling.

"I like it a lot. It's really very, very pretty, really magnificent. Thank you very much."

I go closer to kiss Him but, with a gesture of His hand, He signals me to keep my distance.

"Wait. It's not as easy as that. Things have to be earned. You haven't done anything for me today. You have to show me how submissive you are. I need proof that you're worthy of me."

I look at Him and smile, ready to kneel on the spot and take Him in my mouth, but He stops me.

"You're going to leave the shop, go up to a man, any man, I leave it up to you, and ask him to pay for these things, in return for which you'll suck him off in this fitting room, in front of me. Go on. Now."

I look at Him, stunned, not sure if He's making fun of me.

"I can't do it," I finally blurt out.

He lifts His hand and slaps my face.

"I'm not asking you what you want, I'm demanding that you leave this shop, find a man in the street who'll pay for these frilly things, then suck him here in front of me."

His voice is hard and full of authority. I realize He isn't joking. I'm afraid. Afraid of losing Him. Afraid of disappointing Him. And yet I can't. I'm not a whore, I don't give a damn about this bustier, I want to run away, I can't just walk out into the square, where I've had a hundred business meetings with clients who appreciated the strategies I proposed, and prostitute myself with the first man I meet.

His voice becomes more cajoling.

"Look how beautiful you are, you're gorgeous, it'll be easy. Obey, Élodie, obey. You know you're going to do this for me. I know you're strong enough, I know it excites you. Because you know it excites me, too. Go on, my darling. Obey."

I stand there, unable to speak, unable to say a word. His eyes turn hard. He slaps me again. I raise my hand to my bruised temple.

"Is everything all right, mademoiselle?" the salesclerk calls from behind the curtain, ready to intervene.

"Yes, thank you."

I leave the fitting room like an automaton.

"You look great," says the young woman, but I don't hear her.

◆ ◆ ◆

I turn around, expecting Him to smile and indicate that the game's over, but His face is somber and impenetrable, His gray eyes colder than I've ever seen them before.

I put my head down and cross the shop in a few long strides. Trying not to think, I leave the shop. The customers and the salespeople watch me in amazement.

One of them tries to stop me.

"Leave her," I hear behind me.

The place de la Madeleine is thronged with people.

I've emptied my head of thoughts. In front of me, a group of pedestrians is waiting for the lights to change in order to cross the rue Tronchet.

A man of about forty in a gray suit turns when he sees me. He stares at me in astonishment. "Please, monsieur," I blurt out in a low voice, controlling my sobs, "I beg you, please pay for these things and I'll make it worth your while."

"I'm sorry, mademoiselle, I don't quite understand."

"Please, if you do this, I'll suck you, in the shop, please, don't leave me here like this, I don't have any choice, I have to, please, monsieur, do it."

The man smiles.

"You'll catch cold, my dear. Go home quickly."

He sees my tears.

For several seconds, he looks at me, without saying

anything. I stand there, ignoring the passersby who turn and stare at me in surprise. Tears are streaming down my cheeks and my legs feel weak beneath me.

After what seems an interminable hesitation, the man very gently takes me by the shoulders.

"Come, mademoiselle. You're too pretty to stay here. Something will happen to you."

He pulls me into the shop.

"How much?"

The assistant takes a few moments to regain her composure.

"With the G-string and the stockings, two hundred and eighty-two euros."

He's behind me, watching the scene in silence. I don't even dare look at Him.

The man throws a wad of notes on the counter and strokes my hair.

"Now you're free."

"But I haven't—"

"Please. You're great."

Only now does the man turn and see Him standing there watching us, a thin smile on His face.

The man takes my hand.

◆ ◆ ◆

"If he's your Master, then He doesn't deserve you. Think about it, for me." And he turns on his heels, without even giving me time to thank him.

Like an automaton, I go back to the fitting room to get dressed.

I feel exhausted. I'm shaking all over.

He doesn't join me.

I drop the bustier, the stockings, and the G-string on the floor and dress, trying to think of nothing. I feel sad enough to cry. I leave the fitting room and head for the exit with my eyes down.

"Your purchases, mademoiselle."

The saleswoman has hurriedly picked up the things from the floor and stuffed them in a little white bag.

I take it, thank her, and rush out into the street.

He catches up to me and takes me by the waist.

"You're very beautiful. You're lucky, you got out of it."

He kisses my cheek and I hear Him laugh.

"See you tonight, I'll pick you up at nine. Put those things on under a black dress."

And He goes.

◆

For once, He's taken the trouble to get His car from the parking lot and come to the corner of my street.

I get into His Mercedes convertible and I'm amused to see that He's showing off, sitting in His flashy car with me by His side. Maybe He doesn't think I'm too bad after all.

In accordance with His instructions, I've put on a sober, classic black dress over the Erès set, although, as it consists of several pieces of tulle one on top of the other, it's actually transparent from the waist up. I'm wearing my hair in a bun, held up by a thin black brooch-shaped hair clip, and I've painted my lips a dark color.

No sooner have we left my luxury seventh-floor apartment than He puts His hand in His pocket and takes out a conical object. This time, I know immediately what it's for.

"Put it in. Where you know I like it."

I take hold of the stiff latex.

"By myself?"

He gives me an exasperated look that speaks louder than words. I try to do as He says, but it isn't very practical to stretch my panties with one hand and push the thing, which is dry and tends to stick, into my narrow anus. I wriggle on the dark red leather of the car seat with my legs in an awkward position, aware that more than one surprised motorist is getting an excellent low-angle view of my pelvic region.

The dildo won't go in.

"I'm really sorry, I can't do it."

He purses His lips and doesn't look at me, but at the first red light He tells me to turn my ass toward Him.

Watched by the fortunate driver of the Range Rover next to us, He slips a hand under my buttocks and, without further ado, forces the object inside me, stretching my reluctant sphincter.

I hold my breath in order not to scream.

"But—do you want me to have dinner like this?"

That's another question I shouldn't have asked, and He won't even deign to answer.

When we arrive at the Maison Blanche, I concentrate on pretending to be as relaxed as possible.

Léa and Aurélien are already waiting. They've reserved a table in a little alcove on the ground floor. I hold my breath as we cross the big room, avoiding everyone's eyes. They're clearly startled by my outfit, which defies all the rules of propriety.

No sooner have I sat down than I ask Him to order me some champagne and a simple gazpacho—how could I even attempt to swallow solid food under the circumstances?

He and Aurélien don't know each other, but quickly strike up a conversation. I was right, they have similar ideas on what constitutes their ideal, their paradise of freedom and domination.

They discuss the other women in the restaurant, but I don't understand all their allusions.

I'm enjoying myself, enjoying the submissive role I'm playing.

Léa's flawless twenty-two-year-old beauty has already made an impression, to judge by the insistent looks of the few unaccompanied males within sight. She looks stunning this evening with her short hair, her long, slender legs revealed by a black leather microdress, and her big green eyes, slightly ash brown at the edges. She talks excitedly, getting quickly to the heart of the matter. She tells us how much she hated the Barbar. The sight of all those men and women on display in those small cages, contorting their insipid bodies, covered in cellulite, trying to excite everyone in preparation for what was to come, was more pitiful than anything else. What disappointed her most was how glum these supposed S&M diehards were. Being among like-minded people, they made no attempt to be original, in fact, they seemed quite bored.

"The atmosphere's really quite commonplace. Although everyone's trying to outdo everyone else in the humiliation game, there's no emotion, no sincerity."

On the other hand, she tells us, with all the arrogance

of youth, how she long ago learned to use a whip—even though she doesn't ride—and how happy she is to submit to all of Aurélien's demands and then take shelter in his arms, while he whispers to her as he falls asleep that he loves her as he's never loved anyone else. Aurélien is the love of her life. She knows it. She's sure of it. There'll never be anyone else like him. She'll never give herself to anyone the way she gives herself to him.

The conversation makes me feel a bit sick. I realize I'm giving myself, with all my sincerity, all my integrity, to a man who gives me nothing in return, a man I can't communicate with, a man who'll never show me the slightest gratitude even though, deep down, I hope He'll reach a point where He can't do without the pleasure of my devotion by loving in me the pain He causes me.

My eyes fill with tears when I hear Him tell the others that I'm not His mistress and He's not my lover, that our relationship isn't an affair, that it's all just a game, something fleeting, like the sun before it disappears behind a cloud, and its only rule is to give Him pleasure.

I envy Léa. I envy Aurélien's love for her. I envy the strong ties that bind them, the tenderness of their shared awakenings, their journeys to the depths of the ocean, the books they discover together.

◆ ◆ ◆

This combination of depravity and emotion surprises and excites me, and I question her about it.

Aurélien answers for her, in his harsh, beautiful voice.

"We have a ritual.

"Léa is the woman I love, the woman I respect and pamper. But she's also the woman I've chosen, the woman who's agreed to submit and give me the whole of herself.

"As soon as her name is spoken, a secret name only we know, Léa transforms herself into this other woman, a slave who knows no limits."

What a nice idea! Not Dr. Jekyll and Mr. Hyde, but Madame de Rénal answering to the magic name and turning into O.

His voice jolts me out of my daydreams. He's telling them about our shopping trip to Erès, how I agreed to prostitute myself—and how my client paid without even using my services.

"I think I must punish you. You disobeyed me. That's inadmissible."

I lower my eyes.

"He didn't want to," I murmur, astonished at his dishonesty. "I could hardly chase him down the street and give him a blow job!"

"I see I'm obliged to punish you.

"But first you have to get ready.

"So I'll be grateful if you'll get up, go to the toilet, and come back carrying the dildo you've got inside you, *in your hand*.

"And it's in your own interest to make sure that everyone in the restaurant notices the object; otherwise, I'll make you do the same journey again, crawling on the floor.

"Now."

Aurélien looks at me with great interest, clearly very amused by this new game.

Léa seems quite horrified, but doesn't say a word to save my virtue.

Maybe Aurélien has spoken the "other name" without my noticing.

But He doesn't seem to be joking at all.

I take a deep breath, stand up, and slowly cross the room to the toilets. I know that going there will be easier than coming back.

In the toilets, I don't even bother to close the door of the cubicle. I immediately pull out the oblong cylinder. It's been hurting me so much, it's an enormous relief to be rid of it.

I wash my hands, rinse the object, wipe it on one of the white towels by the side of the toilets, and ponder how I can emerge with honor—if that's the word—from His new game.

It occurs to me to keep the object inside the towel. Everyone will see me crossing the room carrying an object wrapped in a towel, but I doubt that any of the distinguished clientele of the restaurant will ever guess what it is.

It's out of the question for any of these businessmen— whom I might well see again in my office tomorrow morning—to see me cross the restaurant with a dildo in my hand.

The door opens and a woman comes in. I quickly hide the object under the towel, but I still have the impression she gives me a strange look before diving into one of the stalls.

Her presence behind me, and the knowledge that she'll be coming out in a few seconds, makes my mind up for me.

Smiling, and swaying my hips, I walk confidently to my table, holding the towel with the dildo tightly in my right hand.

Aurélien smiles at me, and Léa bursts out laughing, but He doesn't seem to find it funny at all. Maybe He thinks I'm making fun of Him in front of my friends, people He doesn't know. In fact, He seems very angry, and I lower my head.

"Darling"—I jump, and wait for the worst—"I have the feeling you didn't really understand what I asked you to do, unless you find it amusing to make fun of me.

"You leave me no choice but to punish you. Which is

probably what you want anyway. So I demand that you leave this table at once, because I don't want you here anymore, and go and wait for me on the terrace. I'll join you there in a few moments. While you're waiting, think of the punishment that awaits you. Get going!"

The tone of His voice is uncompromising, and I realize He isn't joking. I stand up immediately, ask a waiter how to get to the terrace, and cross the room in my transparent dress, trying hard to appear self-confident, although my soul is on fire.

The view of Paris is amazing. The Eiffel Tower seems to be staring at me, the Invalides mocking me, and the Sacré Coeur smiling at me.

My heart is racing, I don't know if that's a sign of joy or great anxiety, a mixture of the two, I suppose, but I do know my cunt is aching for Him, waiting for Him to come.

I pass my hand over the wrought-iron rail and take a deep breath of the mild late-spring air. The stars look less bright because of the lights of the city. I stand quite still and wait for Him.

To my great surprise, I'm pulled out of my daydream by Léa's mules clicking on the marble floor of the terrace. I turn to her and smile. A few more steps and she's joined me. She hugs me warmly.

"How secretive you are! I didn't know. You never said anything. You should have, you can trust me. How long has it been going on? Anyway, he's magnificent!"

I don't have time to answer her. He's already here. Behind Him, Aurélien, who stands back for a few moments, then joins Léa and puts his arms around her shoulders.

"Kiss her." I turn to look at Him, smile, and bury my face in the back of Léa's neck and kiss her bare shoulders and neck.

She lets me do it, joining her hands behind her back and offering me her tongue and her breasts. Her kisses are languid and sensuous, she arches her back and puts her arms around me. Her perfume is sweet and her mouth a little peppery, her lips are pink and full, her small breasts rise and harden as my fingers search out her nipples.

I savor the pleasure of this sudden intimacy but all I can think about is Him. I know He's two or three steps behind me, watching us. With every move I make, I feel His eyes on me, and that makes me arch my back even more.

I'm overcome with desire. I'd like Him to fuck me right here, right now, in front of Léa and Aurélien, on the terrace of this swanky restaurant.

◆ ◆ ◆

I've forgotten the punishment He promised me. He's loosening His tie, which reminds me of our first encounter, and I turn away from Léa and bend my head toward Him, expecting Him to blindfold me.

But instead, He puts my hands together and crosses them at the wrists and ties them to the wrought-iron balustrade.

Léa is still beside me, kissing my shoulders.

Then I feel Him lift my dress, His hand brushes against my thigh as He lifts the material, which He pulls over my head so that it falls on to my forearms. I realize I'm standing in a bustier on the highest terrace in the avenue Montaigne, with Paris in front of me, and one of the best restaurants in the city behind me.

I feel Aurélien's hands grab my buttocks and I close my eyes, afraid he'll try to fuck me, but my fears aren't realized, all he does is put his fingers first inside my cunt, then inside my enlarged asshole. Then he takes his fingers out and lifts them to my mouth. I lick them with application. His clear skin is as soft as silk. Then Léa hugs us, and in the silence of the night I hear her kisses responding to the man she loves. Aurélien moves away from me and places Léa next to me, her back against the balustrade.

Their embrace is incredibly daring, considering how
high up we are. I watch as he lifts the tight-fitting leather
above her waist and she immediately opens her legs to let
him penetrate her, at a vertiginous angle, on the edge of
the balcony. I can't see how the thin rail can possibly with-
stand the thrusts of his cock as he plunges farther and farther in.

Léa grips his neck, so excited she barely knows what
she's doing. She even throws her head back and arches
her body, balancing on the balustrade, to make it easier
for him to fuck her.

I see her fingers digging into Aurélien's shoulders and
hear her breathing getting faster. All at once he pulls her
to him and turns her around and enters her from behind. I
see the two of them against the starry night. Léa is shaking all over, she puts her left hand between her legs and
starts touching herself, and at the same time grabs my tied
hands with her right hand. The thrusts of Aurélien's cock
inside her are getting faster, but then I see Aurélien grimace and slow down, and I realize he's holding back. I
envy Léa, and I want Him.

But He's still behind me, not even touching me. I can feel
His breathing close to my ear. Aurélien clasps Léa a little
tighter in his arms, and his moans float off into the sky

over Paris. I hear His breathing. He's whispering now.

"Nobody will ever treat you as I'm going to treat you. You'll never forget what I'm going to do to you tonight. You'll never experience anything like it again, you're my bitch and my slave. You belong to me and nobody else. After tonight, you won't know who you are anymore. I'm going to make you suffer, I'm going to make you scream, your body will bear the marks, and although the burning sensation will go away, you'll miss it like a drug. I'm going to give you a beating and you'll love it."

By the time I hear Him slide his belt out of His trousers, I'm in an indescribable state. When I feel the belt sting my buttocks for the first time, I can't hold back a real cry of pain, and when the leather penetrates my skin, leaving a mark on it, I'm barely aware of Aurélien and Léa interrupting their embrace for a moment, smiling, then kissing and continuing where they left off, as if the music of the leather slapping my rump is giving a rhythm to their lovemaking, increasing their desire for each other. My eyes blur with tears, the blows succeed one another with increasing violence, I bite my lips until they bleed in order not to scream in pain, or pleasure, I don't know which it is, I'd like it to stop but I'd also like Him to continue, I'm His, He told me so and now He's proving it to me, He's marking my body and I'm His.

I know He has a hard-on. I don't need to touch Him, I just know.

I'm reduced to purple streaks and a burning sensation, nobody has ever raised his hand to me, I'm petrified and bewitched by the humiliation of my naked, lacerated body; I want to beg for mercy, the pain is unbearable; forgotten images flash into my mind, when I was a child I dreamed I was Snow White, I had a wicked stepmother who whipped me to keep me to line, but I withstood the whipping, defied her with my whole being, each time it happened was another opportunity to prove how strong I was, how superior I was, even though I was much younger than her.

Now I'm giving myself to a man who's showing me He deserves me by beating me, and each blow is more proof of how much He cares about me and how much subservience He demands, and I'm infinitely grateful to Him for it.

My legs won't support me anymore and I collapse, except that I can't collapse all the way because of the way my wrists are tied to the balustrade, and He continues to beat me, now it's the turn of my back and shoulders to bear the brunt, my hair gets caught in the belt as it comes down, and each time He lifts it again tufts of hair get pulled out. It hurts, it hurts a lot, but the pain is doing me good.

I remember what the psychic said. *One day, a woman will get killed.*

I'm not sure that woman isn't me.

I must have fainted. My back and my buttocks are on fire, I'm hanging by my wrists above Paris, and I'm alone.

I dare to whisper His name but He doesn't answer me, and I know He isn't here. I'm alone.

The sky is bright. I become aware of light behind me, and remember I'm at the Maison Blanche. I weep. It hurts. I'm alone and I don't understand, I don't dare call out, I know He's gone, and I must go, too, but when I collapsed, the weight of my body made the bonds on my wrists even tighter and I can't get them loose.

I weep and wait for Him but He doesn't come.

After what seems like an infinity, I finally hear a door open behind me, and hurried footsteps.

"Mademoiselle, mademoiselle!"

A hand touches my shoulder for a moment, and then immediately withdraws.

Of course I say nothing. I don't see the point in explaining to the headwaiter—I'm sure that's who it is—that I'm head over heels in love with a madman who tied me to this rail and whipped me till the blood ran.

I feel a knife tearing the silk, freeing my hands. I try to

stand but my numb, aching body won't respond, I'm lifted up and supported and asked for my name, but I don't give it, I manage to find the strength to demand that they call me a taxi. All I want is to get in it and disappear.

I weep silently, I need to hear His voice and feel His hand on me.

For the next three weeks, I make sure I conceal the marks on my body by going to bed after my husband and always wearing one of those old long white cotton nightdresses with lace fringes and someone else's initials, which I've bought over the years from flea markets or shops selling old linen. Gradually, the wide, telltale streaks on my back fade. Not once has He called to find out how I am.

The only one who inquires about me is Léa. Her kindness wins my trust, and I tell her everything. My description of how the evening ended leaves her speechless. I beg her never to tell anyone what happened.

X

Not a day goes by that I don't torture myself thinking about His studied indifference toward me.

I have nightmares about the line He might try to make me cross, like forcing me to be fucked by other men.

In my dreams, He takes me to a secret place. I'm blindfolded, and dressed all in black leather, He has me on a leash, with a few of His toys hidden in my anatomy. I give in to all His demands. Maybe He spits at me, or makes me crawl to Him and lick inside His ass, plunging my submissive tongue in as far as it will go. He exhibits me, showing everyone what He's made me do, what I do for Him. I'm worthy of Him. He's proud of me.

He hires the services of one of those penniless young Russian women, ready to satisfy all His whims. I choose her, tall with brown hair, shaved all over, perfectly trained. We blindfold her and both suck her and fondle her in a ballet of hands and skins and mouths, it's dark and the music is intoxicating, we lay her on the ground and drip champagne into her navel and lick it off, I kiss Him while she sucks Him, I go from His mouth to His sensitive nipples and suck on them so strongly He hears the sound, the way He likes it.

We take turns sitting on Him and contracting our cunts around His cock, otherwise keeping quite still.

He guesses which one is me and which one is the whore, we're united in our enslavement to Him. He babbles insanely, screams, insults women, moans that He can't do without our cunts. He takes off His blindfold and gives us orders, makes her lick me until I come, sodomizes me while she licks His anus and strokes His balls.

He takes me to a garden where He strips me while unknown men look at me, their cocks pointing in my direction, and masturbate. He lays me down on my back and makes me take other men's cocks in my mouth and cunt and ass.

I try to struggle but He keeps hold of my hands, I try to cry out but He kisses me. His lips are so soft they stifle my protests, my legs are lifted by strangers and held to make me easier to enter, and the men penetrate me one after the other at a phenomenal speed, I can't tell one cock from another. He tames me with His kisses and His whispers: "You're mine, you're at my disposal, you do everything I want, you no longer fully exist."

Then He sticks His cock in my mouth, unless it's someone else's, but I know it isn't because I'd recognize Him anywhere.

And again these unknown bodies penetrate mine, opening my ass and my cunt, knocking against my teeth, my hair is sticky with the sperm spurting over my ass and back and neck and spreading all over my body.

I'd like to scream but I'm His and He compliments me: "I'm proud of you, I've had bitches and trained them, but none like you."

And I tell myself: "I'm His, I exist, I'm His, I'm the woman in His life, He values me because I'm the most submissive and the most devoted."

I wake up suddenly, soaking wet, my cunt and my shoulders and my belly burning like never before.

It takes me a few seconds to realize where I am. I reach out my hand to my husband and touch his shoulders. I recognize his skin and hug him as hard as I can, clinging to his familiar body.

I whisper that I love him, I love him more than anything in the world, he's my balance, the thread that still connects me to life and stops me leaping into the void, into the hell that's been predicted for me.

I think about my baby, who's sleeping peacefully in the arms of his bear, which talks and cries to get attention.

I'm afraid of losing my life, my fragile, precious, comfortable life, but I can't give Him up. He's like a force I can't fight, an inescapable part of my life, even though I thought my life was fulfilled. I don't understand, but I don't even try. All I know is that I'm condemned to devote all my efforts to deserving Him, over and over again.

XI

For the first time, He's invited me to dinner at a friend's. I take His invitation as being tantamount to a promotion, and spend the three days before the dinner, when I'm not working, on the female fripperies that have become indispensable to the way I present myself: I wander the streets at lunchtime in search of the right dress, between visits to the hairdresser, the beautician, the manicurist, and so on.

By seven o'clock on Thursday I feel ready, my fingernails and toenails are impeccably manicured, I've sacrificed the hour I usually spend every day with my beloved mare to have my hair done at Leonor Greyl, and I've even found a little backless dress at Calvin Klein, black lace on a flesh-colored background, which He ought to like.

I feel totally feminine, and if it weren't for the fact that I'm worried about a tricky case I have to plead tomorrow, I'd be ready to throw all caution to the winds. I wait for Him to call, my heart pounding. As the time passes, I feel more and more wound up.

He doesn't call until nine. He asks me to meet Him there, because He's late and doesn't have time to come and pick me up or to wait for me.

So be it. I'll just have to overcome the embarrassment I'm going to feel when I don't arrive on His arm.

I'd never have imagined an apartment like this existed in the rue des Saints-Pères. At the end of a courtyard, there's a kind of art gallery, with immaculately white walls. At the entrance, a huge flat screen showing a silent video, repeated ad infinitum, of a woman dancer who sits speaking inaudible words, passing her hand through her jet-black hair, apparently losing her temper, to judge by the fierce way her lips are moving, while her whole upper body remains stiff and impassive and taut, greeting the young girls as they come in. Yes, there are a lot of young girls here: hardly more than children, only just into puberty, and already so tall and long and sure of the promise of their barely formed breasts. Bare midriffs, hair cut short or flowing over their shoulders, jeans clinging to their bony hips, feet bare or in flip-flops, a whole head taller than me, no eye makeup, pink lips. Too young to be friends of my little sisters' and too old to envy me anything, and very real to these successful men in their forties who are all on the prowl, full of confidence in the power that money brings and the attractions of showbiz dinners, weekends in Essaouria, jetting off for an afternoon in Deauville, an evening at Jimmy's, a night at the Normandy.

At sixteen, I was studying for my exams, and dreaming of myself as a heroine out of Matzneff, but these girls are learning English and dreaming of a future as the idol of some jet-setter.

In the middle of the pop art canvases and Calder-style mobiles and all the other sculptural beauties of iron and skin, I feel as if I'm drowning in a vast white ocean. It's like a diagram of order and disorder, this formal French garden invaded by foliage and other things that are starting to blossom. I feel about as much at ease as my Great Pyrenees dog would feel in a show reserved for greyhounds.

Carried along by this stream of anorexic adolescents, who sway their hips as they come and go, I don't see Him among the guests and feel somewhat at a loss, aware that I'm not attracting anyone's attention, except perhaps by being overdressed and oversophisticated, the only explanation for which is that I'm in my thirties—twice the age of these unreal young madams.

◆ ◆ ◆

The other thing that would allow even a blind person to pick me out from the crowd is that I seem to be the only real Parisienne.

All the men here seem to have developed a sudden passion for Russian, Serbo-Croatian, Romanian, Polish, and Czech—I'm bluffing, of course, I can't tell any of these languages apart!

It suddenly comes home to me how I must have exasperated all the wives of my husband's friends, how arrogant I must have been without realizing it, a very young girl madly in love with a man in his fifties. All those dinners I went to wearing a miniskirt, with my hair down my back and lots of eyeliner like Brigitte Bardot, flaunting my cleavage, greeting the female guests, all of them old enough to be my mother, with an insulting "Hello, madame." Now I understand the hate I felt in their eyes, and my husband's pride as he showed off his young law-student wife.

"Here you are at last. I didn't think you were coming." His solemn voice makes me jump. It's Him! Him! Him!

"But I was here! I've been looking for you for an hour, it was horrible, there are so many people here and I don't know anyone. Oh, if only you knew how happy I am to see you!"

With a spontaneous burst of tenderness—maybe a bit calculated all the same—I hug Him, within sight of as many onlookers as possible.

"Let's keep calm, shall we?" He says, restraining my enthusiasm.

I immediately let go of Him and drown myself in champagne, which a kind man, who must have spotted my confusion, comes and serves me as my glass empties. I'm grateful to him and thank him with a smile, which, while it may not be the prettiest here, is certainly the most sincere.

But He's still by my side. I inquire about the briefs He's been working on, the cases He's won lately. How easy it is to talk to a man about himself, about his own talent, his own success.

Our host, His friend, joins Him, I hear them evaluating the vital statistics and the photographic prospects of the evanescent beauties fluttering through this incredible apartment.

The image of my son keeps coming back to me in flashes, his reproachful look when I left him in his babysitter's arms to come to this party. He could be in my arms, I would read him stories and he'd whisper his first sentences, his first declarations of love, "Mommy, love Mommy, baby love Mommy," repeating back to me the words I've said so often myself when I kiss him before he goes to sleep at night, I'd bury my face in his neck and shoulders and stomach and devour him with kisses, except I'm here at a trendy party full of men displaying the power of money and appearances, and young, slender, fragile foreign girls, each of them determined to find a Pygmalion with the means to take her under his wing and teach her all about Paris and Gucci and Rossi and all those things.

I turn, and He's already gone. The buffet is piled high with big Moroccan salads and tempting *pastillas*. People are taking their places at little round tables, which are supposed to be welcoming.

I can't see Him, maybe He's in the garden, or maybe He's gone to wash His hands, or shut Himself up somewhere to make a phone call. His friend, noticing how disappointed I look, hands me a plate of *pastilla*—he's realized I'm not one of those who've made a solemn vow of starvation—and invites me to sit at a table. Not daring to decline his courteous proposition, I do as he says, but keep my eyes open for Him.

Doing my best to put the extraterrestrials around me off the scent, I try to engage the girl on my left in conversation. She answers in a language I don't understand a word of and smiles regretfully.

I try for a moment to convince myself that in my real life, which isn't this one, I'm extremely privileged: I have a profession that excites me, people who listen to me and pay me to think, an apartment all to myself where I can sleep, a family I can count on.

On my left, a man I'm obliged out of politeness to refer to as *getting on in years* is trying, in perfect English, to convince a feline redhead of the attractions of Gstaad, where he'd really like to take her next weekend, but she says it sounds too cold, brrrr, she'd prefer the Virgin Islands. The conversation is none of my business. He's still not here, where is He, He couldn't possibly have left the party without telling me, He may be a devil but He's well-bred, where is He?

Time's passing and He still hasn't come back, and by now I've eaten the whole *pastilla*. There's no longer even any champagne left, the kind man, my only ally, has made a point of coming and apologizing, I'm clearly very popular with the waiter, I really would have done anything, endured anything, but I wouldn't dare just leave like that, why is He doing this to me?

But just as He vanished, He reappears.

"There's a projection room next door, they were showing a film with Mickey Rourke and Robert De Niro, very interesting. Come to the buffet with me, I'm hungry." As

He piles *mechoui* and cumin-flavored carrots onto his plate, He says: "The only interesting woman here, sexually speaking, is the one from Mauritius sitting on the sofa behind you. Let's go and join her."

And He sits down next to the girl. She's dark, with exceptionally fine features that could have been drawn with a pencil. Her legs are so long she must look like a goddess when she walks—fortunately, she remains seated and spares me the sight. He asks her about her family, wonders what mix of ancestors could have produced such an exceptional creature, asks her what languages she speaks, how did she come to Europe, doesn't she feel cold in winter, how can she bear the arrogance of all these white men who surely haven't missed the opportunity of making her acquaintance, how can she live in this superficial civilization where money makes the world go 'round, how can she manage without the snorkel-free dives, the sea urchins scooped from the rock and eaten raw, the golden sands, the coconut milk?

Meanwhile I keep asking myself why I'm here. I feel less and less at ease, I'm sure this girl isn't for me, He isn't going to share her. Why humiliate me like this? Why bring me into this world? I don't belong in it, I find it perfectly ridiculous, and it doesn't want anything to do with me, with my normal body, my thirty-odd years, my studies, my bourgeois upbringing, the things I'm interested in.

To get up and leave would be an insult, I don't dare, I'm too afraid of losing Him, infinitely afraid that He'll never call me again. But why is He doing this to me? Why has He made me come? Maybe it's a test, to see how much I can tolerate, how far my submissiveness will go.

I say nothing and stay where I am, listening in silence, as if I weren't here. I just don't want to leave Him to her, not yet, that would be too easy. I want Him to leave with me on His arm, I want her to know He's mine, at least a little bit mine.

Their conversation continues, I've never heard Him talk so much, or seem so interested. Is this His usual method of seduction?

Will He blindfold her, too, one day, and whisper in her ear the thrilling words that enslaved me?

Does she even know who she's dealing with, who she has the honor of talking to, how painful it is for me to watch Him seduce her? I thought I knew that I wasn't allowed to be jealous, I thought I knew that I have no exclusive rights to Him, but now, suddenly, I feel a kind of diffuse pain spreading through my body. All I want is for Him to get up and take me away from here, anywhere, just so that He can order me to suck Him and make Him come. He could stick all the dildos in the world inside me, ask me for anything, just as long as we're away from here, away from her, because it turns me on to see Him get a hard-on, because I'm ready for anything just to make sure His desire is only for me.

But He doesn't look at me, it's as if I'm not even here, as if I no longer exist. I'm just an onlooker at my own downfall, usurped by a black bombshell with raised breasts that challenge the world with their arrogance. The pain is sharper now, it's going right through me, I've drunk too much champagne again, but what else can I do?

Their words, their laughter, are torture to me, I'm overwhelmed by my own powerlessness. All at once I come to a decision, and immediately stand up.

"Good night. I have to go, it's a little late, you know how it is, the babysitter."

She does know how it is, and shows a touch of female solidarity, though it turns out badly for me.

"I have to go, too. I have a casting call tomorrow morning. I live in the rue Saint-Honoré. Could either of you give me a lift?"

"Of course," He cries. "Let's go!"

And here was I secretly hoping, only a moment ago, for something to happen, a tussle on the stairs, in a doorway, in the car, just one single contact, just one touch, anything to give me back my old status, make me feel I'm alive again.

But we're already in the hall, and He's looking for His coat and the Burberry she's asked for. I get my leather raincoat and put it on by myself and open the door myself and find myself on the threshold. He doesn't even see me, hasn't realized that I'm leaving, that I've already left, He only has eyes for that incredible black body that is coming closer to His, I mutter an inaudible "good night" and run down the stairs alone and find myself in the street, where I walk up and down the sidewalk looking for my car. I feel sick, there's a real pain penetrating me, spreading through my body, working its way deep inside, gradually blackening my heart and my soul and every one of my intestines, because I'm His, I feel like His thing, like a neglected animal, left in a highway rest area while its owner drives off, unconcerned, far into the distance, but why must He insult me like this?

My eyes blur, blinded with tears. The pain cuts deep into me like a blade. I start the windshield wipers of my car even though it isn't raining. I want to sleep. I want to vomit.

I return alone to my big, cold apartment, thank my son's babysitter, and look for my husband. As usual he isn't here, he's away traveling. Why? Why? I need him so much, his presence, his proximity, his smell in the bedroom, the contact of his skin in the bed, but the bed has been desperately empty for nearly three weeks.

I tiptoe back into my baby's room, as I do every night, and lean over the side of his cot and kiss him and tell him I love him more than anyone, I love his gentle breathing and his tiny nose and his closed eyes and his collection of dummies.

I can't bear to be without him. I lift him up and take him to my bed. I'm going to sleep by his side, cradled in his little arms.

XII

I arrive at the Luxembourg on my little vanilla-colored Vespa, after riding hell for leather. I don't even bother to chain it to the railings, just remove my helmet, take the pin out of my hair, give my almost willowy figure the once-over, and try to catch my breath as I punch in the entry code, which so few people know.

It's 4:20 in the afternoon. I rushed out of the Palais de Justice as soon as I heard His message on my answering machine: "Come. Now. I want you." Just that, nothing else.

His secretary makes me sit down and asks me politely which case we're meeting about. I reply, as seriously as I can, that it's a new case and I've come to talk to Him about it in the hope that He'll agree to work on it with me.

She smiles at me, satisfied with my explanation.

I'm amused to see how much respect she has for our profession, especially when I think of the real purpose of my visit: if only she knew that in a few minutes, behind that door . . . Maybe He'll blindfold me, like the first time, maybe He'll stick strange objects inside me, and if He wants me to, I'll suck Him to the last drop until He throws his head back with a grimace, His fingers digging into my hair.

I've got to this point in my reflections when He opens the padded door of His office and comes striding out toward me, holding out His hand: "My dear colleague, do come in!"

I take His hand and shake it and follow Him into His office, which is lined wall to wall in thick black soft-pile carpet.

I look around me, and am surprised to notice a big dark painting, almost entirely black except for slight differences of texture and material, which I don't recall seeing before.

"Do you like it? It's a Richter."

I nod and remark that what really knocks me out is the photograph to the right of His desk showing a thin, pale young woman with big, bright eyes, wearing tiny green panties and standing very straight, her legs barely parted, against an immaculate background, which I recognize from having seen it in a gallery in Saint-Germain des Prés.

"That photo's amazing. The girl's really beautiful . . . her body's incredible."

"I know. It's Helen. We're going to have a child one day."

Obviously. I lower my eyes, somewhat disconcerted that He's confided in me. I never ask Him questions about His private life.

I'm sure He senses my embarrassment. He asks me to sit down.

I sit facing Him and cross my legs high and smile.

"You haven't done your nails."

My only reply is to blush. I don't dare to point out that since I've been riding every day . . .

Silence.

He stares at me. He seems to be examining every detail of my body, this body He's sent for in such a high-handed way. He knows this flesh, these curves, are His, even though He hasn't yet seen fit to make use of them.

"I'm going on vacation tomorrow for a month. I'm taking Helen to an island somewhere in the Pacific.

"I want you to do something for me. Every night before you go to bed, I want you to remember that you're mine, that I can do anything I like with you, that you belong to me and nobody else, and that as long as I want it, as long as I want you, you'll satisfy all my demands.

"I want you to savor your enslavement to me, and I want you to know that one day I'll give you back your freedom, I'll finally cut the ties that bind you to me, and that from that day on, you'll weep when you remember the pleasure of waiting, the blows I gave you, the way your body was marked and stretched, the rough way I treated you, the way nobody else will ever dare treat you."

I close my eyes. His words permeate my body, my whole being is tense with wanting Him, I quiver deep inside, where I'm most sensitive, most fragile, most dependent, and this dependence has me spellbound, because it's so closely linked to His desire, which is alive and mortal, like a butterfly that will inevitably die when the sun goes down.

"Every night," He goes on, "I want you to beg me to come back to you, I want you to imagine my hands on you, the strength of my cock inside you, even though I haven't yet felt like bestowing that honor on you, you haven't deserved it yet, maybe one day you'll be worthy. I demand that every night, before you go to sleep, you think of me and masturbate, I want you to close your eyes and feel me looking at your cunt." He stops, and stares at my legs with His dark eyes. "Open!!! I want to see you, I want you to feel my eyes on you. Masturbate. Masturbate now, in front of me. I'm watching you."

I freeze. I've always been too modest to indulge in that kind of exhibitionism. He insists: "Masturbate. Open your legs wide and masturbate. Pull your panties down and masturbate. Open wider, I want to see."

Shyly, I do as he says.

"Open wider, I want to get a better view. Look into my eyes. I want to see your eyes when you masturbate, I want to see your eyes flutter and your lips twist and your pretty face distort as the pleasure mounts, look at me, you're beautiful, keep your eyes on mine while I watch your fingers in your cunt as you masturbate, go on, don't stop, feel the heat rising inside you, the tingling sensation in your lower back, the sweat breaking out; your heart pounding faster."

His hard gray eyes bore into me, I have the impression they're taking possession of my whole trembling body. Discreet as I am, I find myself opening my legs to Him and showing Him my fingers moving, turning, spiraling, doing the most intimate, most degrading things right here, in front of Him, the sole witness of my solitary orgasm, showing Him my hands, moistened by my own saliva, as they explore my insides, and I dare to look Him straight in the eyes as He stares at me. He's standing there, calm and collected, not even touching Himself. Does He even have a hard-on? I'm going to come, I want to turn Him on, give Him a hard-on, my legs apart, tensing, twisting, my body swaying, I've never even watched myself in the mirror, never seen the pleasure mounting, reaching its climax, overwhelming me.

I bite my hand to stifle my cry, and He smiles at me.

My body feels broken in pieces but I answer His smile with my eyes.

I've done it, and ridiculous as it may seem, absurd as it may seem, I'm very proud of myself, for masturbating in an office in the afternoon, in front of a man, in front of Him, while He watched me, followed my every move, my every expression, my every wanton action.   ·

Somehow, I find the strength to slide to the ground and crawl the short distance to the armchair where He's been sitting to see me better and put my face on His crotch. I feel His cock inside His trousers, feel it quiver beneath my cheek.

"Please let me make you come."

It's a prayer, a supplication, a harsh whisper, the lament of a woman bewitched and abandoned, kneeling before her God, before the devil, but He's imperturbable, doesn't even deign to answer her, He just gets up, wishes me a nice holiday, reminds me of His instructions, and pushes me out of His office without so much as a kiss.

I leave His office with only one thought in my mind: I have to see Him again.

XIII

Saint-Tropez is a bit of a trial this summer.

I'm sharing a gorgeous house with my best friends, almost on top of the sea. Every morning I take my son to the beach. We set off hand in hand, carrying spades and rakes and a little bucket filled with mussels in our free hands, and when we reach the burning sand he holds out his arm and says, "Mommy! Hot!" and I grab hold of him and carry him, burying my nose in his soft little neck. The lovely Claire, who consults me almost every day on the validity of the strategy she's been pursuing for nearly eight months to seduce the man she's set her sights on, joins us with her little Marie, and we jump up and down on the wet sand as the waves lap around us, and build a few Sleeping Beauty castles, which

Marie quickly razes to the ground with her rake, obviously she doesn't believe in fairy tales, and my son cries and I console him, or at least try to, and he rolls in the water and loses his hat, and I run to him, splashing, and we laugh till we're breathless; and his pacifier falls in the sand, and he shakes it and dips it in the water, which means that now it's too salty, but luckily, the babysitter-cum-guardian angel who looks after all the little princes turns up just then and calms the storm by rinsing the pacifier in clear water, and my baby and I laugh. And then I think about Him, and I slip off my bathing suit and check how my tan is coming along, I'm tanning myself for Him. In the afternoons, there's a summit meeting of all these respectable women, whose fantasies of perfection are modeled on *Madame Figaro.* I look at my friends and listen to them talking, but all I think about is Him.

Last Monday, I found out from a friend who met Him in the corridors of the Palais de Justice that He's already back from His island and has been spending a few days in Paris, dealing with one of His cases.

After much hesitation, I leave a message on His answering machine: "I've got my tan at last. I may have to go back to my office on Tuesday or Wednesday. I'd be really happy to see you. Call me back if you think it's possible and if you want to."

◆ ◆ ◆

The hours and days that follow are unbearable. He doesn't bother to call me back.

I remember the psychic's prediction: *He has no feelings for you. All he thinks about is sex*—and my blood freezes.

Where is He now? Maybe on the Île de Ré, with His Helen and His friends Philippe and Henry—He's talked to me about them but I don't know them. How are they spending their days, what are they eating, who are they sleeping with? Does He ever think about me? Will I ever see Him again? Why didn't He want to see me last week when I suggested going back just for Him?

There's nothing I can do. Just listen to the South American music I heard in his office and think about Him, just about Him, keeping myself going with my memories of Him, recalling the tone of His voice, imagining the letter I'd write to Him, if only He were human, if only He were sensitive, if only He were the kind of man who'd respond to the words I'd write Him, the emotions I'd confess to Him, but I know the Devil has no soul and I can never touch Him, never reach Him, and I have to be content with nothing, with waiting, with indifference, with the thought that maybe one day His desire for me will return, for a reason I'll never understand, or maybe for no reason at all, and with the absurdity of this affair which isn't an affair.

I have to convince myself that there's nothing I can do. Just wait. Wait for Him.

I have to try to take advantage of my vacation, I have to laugh and enjoy myself and not think too much. I have to pass the time, despite the insistent pain of His absence, the total lack of news. Imagining His arms around Helen or someone else, His lips on other lips.

I have to cling to His instructions, which are my only link with Him. Hide myself away and plunge my finger into my empty cunt. Empty of Him. Scorned by Him.

Our arrival at the Voile Rouge beach in Saint-Tropez the first time, the very first time: the way the men look at our plunging bikinis and lick their lips, the way they shake the magnums of champagne between their thighs, the way the bubbles explode and stream over our bodies, an unreal homage, vulgar and comical, to our arrival in this temple of money and debauchery.

The endless, insistent Eastern-style music in the late afternoon, the drunkenness, the weird cocktails, the incredible girls with their surreal breasts, as round as they're high, and their full lips and clear skins, desire is the watchword in this ghetto of money and drugs, and I only have to feel a damp hand on my back to think about Him again, and I see my friends, Inès and Claire, both so beautiful and so innocent, so attached to their image and their reputation, staring wide-eyed at this world that isn't theirs and isn't mine.

We watch it all in amazement—the men arching their backs and swaying their hips, cigars bobbing up and down in the corners of their mouths, the young and not-so-young women, sirens with breasts raised to the sky, defying all the laws of gravity, the money evaporating in streams of champagne poured over tanned skins—and we sniff these new smells cautiously, these cocktails of alcohol and sweat, and look at one another and smile, staggered by such an excess of vulgarity.

And yet this place, where all that matters is sex and depravity, actually seems quite dull. To me, these men showing off, these women with their naked bodies, are the very opposite of eroticism. I look at them, convinced that none of them has ever experienced, or will ever experience, the things He's introduced me to.

Right now I have no doubt of my superiority, and I feel sure I have nothing to envy these babes who don't know which breast to show first to attract the attention of the assembled males. I look at all these people, how amazed they would be if I told them about my other life, about all the things I've been through. Maybe one day I'll write about it.

And then I look at these girls with their surreal figures, who look as if they've been drawn by Manara, and I can't help imagining them in my place, confronting Him. Would they, too, have dived in? Why did He choose me? How did He know? Does He treat His other mistresses the same way? I can't get these questions out of my head.

There's only one thing I know for certain. He was right when He said no one else will ever treat me like Him.

Géraldine wants to get a divorce! My Géraldine, faithful, sweet determined Géraldine, so sure of her marriage, so utterly devoted to her family, threatens to put an end to it all because once again her husband is in the middle of a huge property deal and can't join her. Claire and I try in vain to console her. All her husband ever does, she retorts, is work and work at his acquisitions, and money's no compensation. We try to tell her that although it may not be compensation, it's a definite comfort, and urge her to test our theory by going straight to the place des Lices and robbing it blind.

Reluctantly, she agrees to do as we say and leaves for town with Achille's American Express card, determined to follow the instructions of us two shopaholics always living beyond our means, and comes back with nothing but a pair of glasses, Chanel admittedly, but glasses all the same! The three of us burst out laughing at such good taste.

I slaughter my eternal suitor Étienne at backgammon, winning almost enough to buy a bathing suit. His excuse is that he's not feeling like himself, without knowing why.

The following night, he returns with a pretty Russian girl on his arm, who keeps herself hyped up by rushing into the bathroom every eight minutes, and boasts that she's spending the whole summer in the microcosm of Saint-Tropez showbiz without any fixed abode. She's living with him right now, at least until Thursday, but it could be longer if they get along.

Once his hormones have been assuaged, Étienne gets his revenge at backgammon.

I preferred him unattached.

It's Inès's birthday. She's a stunning girl, and I really like her a lot. She's so beautiful and so impressive when you meet her for the first time, and so open and generous when you take the trouble to get to know her. I buy her a little Gucci bag, which her fiancé Raphaël thinks is a good choice. In the shop, we see a kind of metal belt, which is quite suggestive. Raphaël ties me to the rack. We both burst out laughing. I think about Him. I think how much I've changed, how my view of life has been transformed.

Tonight, Gwenaëlle, who's a real Parisienne, throws a party in Saint-Tropez. I eat four raw carrots and drink several glasses of champagne. All I think about is Him. The Brazilian music turns quite sexy, and as I dance I put my arms around a pretty brunette answering to the name of Sixtine. I know He'd like her, there's a gleam in her eyes that suggests a taste for the pleasures of the senses. Étienne, who's also here, can't believe his eyes. I know he thinks I'm capable of lots of things, but all the same he seems amazed at what I'm doing with this girl. I revel in my provocation, and when the girl, who's clearly in a somewhat advanced state of drunkenness, lets herself go and drops her head on my shoulder, I put my lips on hers. She's startled at first, then returns my kiss. Our tongues meet. The surprise I see in the eyes of the people around us is quite pleasing. I feel very proud that I can shock this gathering of self-satisfied pseudotrendies. I think about Him, I think He'd be pleased with me; maybe I'll get the opportunity to tell Him about it, if only He gives me the chance to see Him again, to spend just a little more time with Him, I hope He'll be thrilled with the results of His training, with the things I'm now capable of even when He's not there, even without His commands, for which I'd give ten years of my life, provided He sends for me again, provided He still wants me.

All I think about is Him.

I notice a tall redhead at the back of the room who can't take her eyes off me. Soon, intrigued by her increasingly insistent look, I let go of Sixtine and am heading for the buffet to try to get an umpteenth glass of champagne when the unknown redhead offers me hers, which is still full. I accept and thank her with a smile. She's an incredible-looking girl, with wild, vaporous hair almost down to her buttocks, legs that look as if they've been cut with a laser, a triangular face with lots of freckles, and big green eyes. I feel as if I've seen her somewhere before. When I ask her, she laughs. "Maybe in the last issue of *Elle,*" she answers, with the hint of an English accent. "I was on the cover."

Her name is Ingrid, and she speaks perfect French. She knows hardly anybody at this party, and she's a little bored. On the whole, she finds the people here too refined and lacking in imagination. She becomes talkative, telling me that she's only passing through, doing photos for a big cosmetics company, and that she's going back to Paris in a few days. She's been living there for four years with her husband, who works in a French bank. She met him at an art gallery in New York. She'd been posing for an artist who was into bondage and liked to photograph women tied up.

I take her out onto a little patio, where it's quieter. I'm captivated by her exceptional looks, and amused by her chattiness and her spontaneity.

Why is she confiding all these things to me? She doesn't even know me.

I think about Him. He'd like her.

I'm already wondering how to take her to Him while she continues telling me about her life, how tough the casting sessions are, how difficult the constant traveling is, often long distances for the sake of fashion shows or photo shoots in the sun, how pleased she is to get back to her husband, who also travels a lot because of his work. They've both been dreaming about having a baby for nearly two years, but they spend so little time together, they haven't been able to conceive yet, this desire for a child won't go away, in the meantime she's looking for a bit of imagination, because the world's so boring.

I can relate to her confessions. Life is strange. What are we both doing at this smart party? Why do we both feel this undeniable attraction for the other?

Why did she approach me? Why did she confide in me right from the start? Maybe it was the way I was behaving with Sixtine. Just as I'm wondering about that, she asks me if I often kiss girls.

"No, not often," I reply, with a naturalness that surprises even me. "It's just that I've been taking a course for the past few months, and I need to keep in training."

I've been thinking so hard about Him, it does me good just to evoke Him.

She laughs, revealing perfect teeth, and confesses to me, I don't know why, that there are so many things she'd like to try, so many things she dreams of being initiated into. Her husband, Godefroy, is wonderful, but they don't get much time together, though they do manage to meet up at least one weekend a month at the house they've bought on Formentera. But they have so little time to see other people, so few mutual friends, there are so many things they'd like to discover together—"life's so short," she says. And all the while I'm wondering how I could involve this gorgeous girl in our games. He'd be so proud of me. I'd like to be able to prepare her for Him, take her to Him, He'd be crazy about her, the three of us would love one another.

Étienne, intrigued by my statuesque companion, decides to join us. I smile at him and, entering into the spirit of the game, introduce them to each other and slip away.

Later, Ingrid slips her cell-phone number into my hand, kisses me on the corner of the lips, and leaves on Étienne's arm. My supposedly bashful admirer clearly has more cards up his sleeve than I suspected. A curious feeling of jealousy creeps up on me as I watch them leaving hand in hand.

If only He loved me a little, just a little. I'd be prepared to do anything just to have that illusion.

I put my new friend's number in my address book and promise myself I'll call her as soon as I get back. For Him.

My little boy is dying to jump into the pool like his idol Sidonie, not realizing that Sidonie is at least three years old and has had six months of advanced swimming classes at the Polo. I hold him by his fingertips, but although he's wearing swimmies, he swallows a mouthful of water. He spits it out again angrily, and I hug him and get him to swim on my back. He grips my hair. My baby, my joy.

Afternoon by the side of the pool. All women.

I chat with Inès.

She's so beautiful, with her slender legs, her willowy figure challenging all standards of measurement, her wide pink mouth, her fine features, her aristocratic distinction. She's very excited about her wedding, which is planned for next summer at Ménerbes, and tells me how happy she is with Raphaël. She'd never be able to understand what's happening in my life, and I'd never be able to tell her about it.

My husband has finally joined us for the weekend. I let him make love to me very tenderly and think about Him. I grip the sheet, thinking about His cock, which has never been inside me.

The "office" opens for business at Sénequier's and all those in search of the best dish on the peninsula get down to work, discussing what happened last night, the look Fabrice X. gave Aurore T., Julie B.'s mad crush on Eddy R., the extraterrestrial creatures they rubbed shoulders with at the Voile Rouge and whether or not they've had boob jobs.

I think about Him.

I'm fascinated by an article in *Marie Claire* in which a number of readers talk about their experiences in swingers' clubs. Not one of them has the courage to confess she might have experienced any pleasure. I smile. What a pity they didn't think of interviewing me, I'd have had a few things to tell. I want Him. I want His challenges. I realize how dependent I am.

I remember a quotation from Matzneff: "The gods are like men, they only really die when they have stopped being loved." So He must be immortal.

I watch a woman strolling in the harbor at eleven in the morning, in stiletto heels and cocktail dress, cell phone stuck to her ear, her high spirits matched only by her vulgarity, an ex-secretary promoted to the rank of shipowner's wife.

Étienne, maybe because he wants me to forgive him for having a new girlfriend who doesn't leave him alone for a single second—which means we never get together and don't have the chance to play backgammon—gives me a book in which the heroine is tied to a tree and raped. Well, well, he knows me better than I thought.

I buy a very short gray-blue silk dress, almost like a nightie. The color reminds me of His eyes. If only He gives me the opportunity to show it to Him.

My friend Sara always tells me that clothes are a useless investment and rarely recoup their cost. I think of my collection of bustiers from Chantal Thomass, La Perla, Cadolle, and Dior, which I've put together in a few months for Him and which He's never done the honors to—never even glimpsed.

My son is playing with Sidonie, under the watchful eyes of his babysitter-cum-nanny. I say I'm feeling very sleepy, but it's an excuse to be alone in my big, cool room. I put my hand between my parted legs and think about Him. I close my eyes and remember His eyes on me the last time; how He watched me touching myself, my middle finger turning, getting bolder, moistened by my own saliva, His eyes looking deep into mine; how He smiled when my orgasm swept over me and I was carried away into an unreal world of uncontrollable spasms.

I dream about His cock inside me, I imagine it forcing its way into my cunt, withdrawing and switching to my ass, moving in and out, I remember an image from the film *Je t'aime, moi non plus,* when she's on the bed and the man who didn't like women forces open her buttocks as roughly as she was expecting, and she screams. I'd like Him to make me scream, too. But why won't He fuck me? Why, why, why? I close my eyes and imagine His hands on my hips, His fingers digging into my flesh, His stomach beating against my buttocks while He's deep inside me, held tight by my incensed entrails, my finger between my teeth, bitten till it bleeds to stifle the vulgarity of an uncontrolled cry. My body convulses with long spasms.

Another visit to the Voile Rouge beach. The grand arrival of
the cruise ship *Riva* some sixty feet from the beach, where
the booming bass of the Eastern-style techno music can
already be heard. The shuttle pulls up, and Inès and I jump
on. There are already two men on board, both not yet tanned.

Raphaël says he'll swim out and join us over there, and
dives in. As the Zodiac speeds toward the landing stage,
one of the two passengers says something to the other, I
can't understand a word of whatever language he's speaking, but it reminds me of the party in the rue des Saints-
Pères. Then the second man reaches into a waterproof bag
and takes out a wad of dollars so thick he can barely hold
it in his hand and gives it to his acolyte, who stuffs it in
his swimming trunks. Inès and I look at each other in
amazement. It's a strange world.

A few budding supermodels are vigorously hopping up and
down on the wooden platform, which vibrates beneath them.
Their breasts, barely concealed by skimpy triangles of cloth,
are a true offense to the laws of gravity. After two glasses of
the really heady orange cocktail that seems to be the trendy
drink of the place, and a few jets of champagne judiciously
directed at our thighs, we join the wild huntresses.

A man has planted himself behind me and is moving my hips in rhythm with his. I can see his black hand on my stomach and feel his erect cock against my lower back. Gently but firmly, I take his hand away and extricate myself from his embrace.

I think about Him. I belong to Him and nobody else.

Raphaël makes a show of coming to my rescue, and I thank him, touched by how protective he is. If he knew what's been happening in my life, what I'm capable of, I don't suppose he'd be so kind to me.

Several glasses later, we're back on the shuttle, speeding away from that incredible beach whose only merit is to be both the most vulgar and the most comical place in the world, a couple of elegant men dressed in Ralph Lauren suggest we take a pass on Raphaël's elegant boat and come on board their yachts, which are no ordinary yachts. Inès and I thank them with a smile, aware that our lives could have been transformed: lawyers and bathing beauties—at last a way to go shopping on the avenue Montaigne without batting an eye!

I think about Him. I know He'd have liked to be with us. He'd have liked to love us in this hot, sexy part of the Mediterranean.

A party in Saint-Tropez full of tanned Parisians. High heels in the sand and hippie-style designer dresses.

Cigars and cocaine, conspicuous signs of success.

Gonzague, who lives in La Baule with his wife and four children, is chatting up the sexy Sixtine.

I watch them with amusement. His mating ritual is about as delicate as a male gorilla's in front of a female gorilla in heat. Sixtine throws me a desperate look.

Giving her no time to change her mind, I put my arm around her waist and move my other hand over the curve of her shoulder and then her stomach.

None of the people around us seem offended by two women getting it on together like this, except maybe Gonzague, who tries to come between us as we dance body to body.

Sixtine's eyes beg me not to abandon her.

I advance my face toward hers and bury it in the curve of her bare neck. She gives me her mouth, which I deign to accept. I think about Him.

◆ ◆ ◆

Gonzague steps back, surprised and disappointed by the advantage I'm taking. I think about Him, about what He's taught me, His training. I feel that He's put His mark, His seal, on me.

Stimulated by my rival's discomfiture, and amused by my conquest's growing excitement, I increase the intensity of my kisses, slip the strap of her thin dress off her tanned shoulder, and quickly put my hand into her cleavage.

I don't have any real desire for the girl. I'm playing. I've started to understand the attraction of playing games. A shiver runs through me. What about Him? What if it's only a game for Him? All at once, I feel sick, I feel ill, I want to get out of here.

Gonzague's appalled look brings me back to reality, and to his "prey," who's snuggling in my arms. Her forwardness surprises me. Actually, when I think about it, I find it disappointing. I think I'd like it better if she resisted a bit more, or at least pretended to.

I'm afraid. I see myself with Him, giving up every one of my desires, anticipating every one of His orders. What if it was all too easy? What if He'd have liked me to resist Him? What if the completeness of my submission didn't excite Him but bored Him instead?

I'm afraid. Infinitely afraid of losing Him.

Sixtine, drunk with champagne, and maybe also with the effects of being celibate for too long, is increasingly uninhibited. Her body moves in time to mine, as my hands knead her flesh almost mechanically.

She gives little moans, which I interpret as encouragement, my tongue burrows farther into her mouth and my hand moves up her thighs.

When I reach her cunt, I discover she's not wearing any panties. She's also very moist. I realize what a strange situation I'm in.

I whisper in her ear that we've become the center of attention. The people at this party, who can boast of being on the barricades in 1968, seem quite shocked.

As commandingly as if I were Him, I pull her toward the house. I want to get her alone on a sofa.

I don't intend to take no for an answer. But far from resisting my caresses, she gives me her body, pressing it against mine, then throwing the top part of her body back against the canvas sofa and opening her legs as wide as possible, offering me her cunt. I look at her and smile— she doesn't notice the touch of mockery.

I think about Him, and about the power of possession.

I look at her and smile and touch her cunt and my fingers are soon wet with her juices, and she arches her back, pushing the mouth of her vagina toward me.

Accepting her entreaties, I relieve her frustration by sticking my mouth into her and searching for her clitoris with my tongue.

I suck her and lick her and think about Him, about what I'm doing without Him, about what He's made me capable of. I've become a well-trained, self-disciplined animal, thanks to the enslavement He's seen fit to bestow on me, the enslavement I've become so dependent on.

Sixtine's cry is stifled by the cushion she's used to cover her face so as not to see me, to forget that it's a woman who's sucking her, that this is the first time a woman has given her an orgasm. She digs her fingers into my hair, which lies across her round belly, then sits up and hugs me as tight as she can and tells me she loves me, it was amazing, unforgettable, unique, better than with a man, she's never felt anything like that before, and I smile and thank her for her compliments and savor the pleasure of domination.

XIV

The vacation's been great, but I'm impatient for it to end. I've been cruising through the days like a boat slicing through water, no longer content with the pleasure of the sun on my skin and the water between my legs and the dinners and the men getting excited and the women confessing.

The days are passing and I belong to Him. I need His smell and the touch of His skin and His commands.

I'm bored, the hours follow one another, I recall His voice, I'm waiting for Him, and reveling in the wait.

To pass the time, I try to take care of myself. I keep track of my tan, have myself massaged with relaxing oils, every day my skin is becoming smoother and more bronzed, I hope He'll like me.

◆ ◆ ◆

Through all these long weeks, He's called me just once, to ask about who's in the house. It seemed as if He was ready to come here. I'll never know what attracted him: Saint-Tropez or my mouth.

Our reunion in Paris is steamy. For once, He forgives my absence with kisses. He wants me to be free tomorrow night.

Indescribable joy. I feel alive again.

I want to surprise Him, think of things before He does. I want Him to know I understand Him.

I call the beautiful Ingrid and invite her to dinner. Luckily, her husband is still away, and she's alone for a few days. It's better that way.

I invite her to join "us" tomorrow night, explaining that I won't be with my husband, I'll be with a friend who's "a bit of a devil" but whom I'm sure she'll like. She laughs and accepts the invitation, without asking any questions.

◆ ◆ ◆

I think about Him. All I think about is Him.

I insist that Ingrid wear a skirt. She laughs and agrees, without asking why. I don't know if she's understood, but she seems to be well disciplined. I'm sure He'll like her.

We arrange to meet at the Café de la Mairie at nine o'clock. I promise Him a surprise. He laughs and tries to find out who, what, how, but I manage to fend Him off.

After hesitating for a while, I decide to wear the gray-blue slip dress I bought on vacation. My hair is longer and lighter in color, my legs are tanned and slim in their flip-flops, my eyes as light as His are dark. I'm feeling quite confident.

I'd like to make Him love me tonight, I'd like Him to know how unconditionally devoted to Him I am. I'd like Him to fuck me, too, to deign to possess what He's scorned so far. Then I'd belong to Him. Then He'll have had everything of me. My soul. And my body.

I imagine the look on His face when He sees this incredible girl.

I feel she's ready. I remember the expression on her face as she watched me kissing Sixtine, and how she immediately approached me. I've imagined her touching herself, I've thought about my hands on her.

I arrive at the place Saint-Sulpice on my scooter. I'm on time. He's already waiting. From the stares I've been getting from the drivers along the quais, I know how good I look, I know the preparation was worth it.

He's on the phone. He smiles and hugs me, and continues His conversation. Just the pressure of His arm around my shoulders as He presses them against His chest moves me more than I can say. Maybe one day, in some small way, I'll be able to make Him feel He can't do without me.

Without actually listening to His conversation, I gather He's asking someone else to join us tonight. When He hangs up, he confirms that He's invited a friend of His, someone I don't know.

"Philippe. I've known him for fifteen years. He only has one fault—he's right-wing. He works at the Élysée." That's all I'm going to find out. For the moment.

I'm a bit disappointed. Three was a good number.

I don't want another man, and I'm afraid the gorgeous Ingrid will be embarrassed or maybe a bit less comfortable than if there were just two of us devoting ourselves to her.

Of course I don't say anything, and keep fending off His insistent questions about the nature of my surprise, as we sit down on the café's uncomfortable chairs. I feel a little tense, and order a glass of champagne. I hope she'll show up. Before long, I'm feeling dizzy.

After a few minutes of polite conversation about our respective vacations, we're joined by a tall man in his forties with a pale complexion and drawn features. He has the earnest look of an overworked civil servant.

They both stare at the young women passing, and question me about my surprise. I keep my answers vague. I even have a bit of fun lying: "She's a doctor, short, a bit ordinary, a bit plump, but very extroverted."

I can tell He's worried, He throws me a reproving look as he listens to my description, then leans toward me and whispers in my ear: "If she isn't worthy of me, I'll beat the hell out of you."

His words make me tremble. I close my eyes for a moment. I'd like Him to fuck me here, right now, to plunge into me in a single movement. I'd like Him to hurt me. I'd like His teeth on my breasts. I'd like Him to bite my neck and my buttocks. Maybe also take off His leather belt and beat me as hard as I know He can.

I've stopped listening to His conversation with Philippe.

I sit upright in my chair, with my legs crossed high, not knowing what to do with my hands as one cigarette follows another.

I feel I'm His, totally, unreservedly.

Just as the boys are starting to lose patience, I see the stunning Ingrid crossing the square toward the café, looking for me. I don't move. I wait for her to spot me among the tourists enjoying the summer evening, and the moment she sees me and gives a big wave, I turn and look at Him as He watches this statuesque girl walking toward us with her long catlike strides.

The excitement in His eyes tells me I was right: my friend is absolutely to His taste.

I notice she's wearing a skirt, and I smile. Good, she's followed my instructions. I guessed she had a strong desire for freedom, and I was right.

I can already imagine her in my arms.

◆

We dine on the terrace of a little restaurant in Saint-Germain. I don't feel hungry, and make do with seven slices of tomato, which amuses Him.

I know He knows all this is only for Him, only to please Him.

The conversation is lighthearted, amusing, and suggestive. Philippe can't take his eyes off me. I'm afraid he wants me and that He'll grant his wish by lending me to him. The two friends seem very close, but I sense that Philippe is gentler—more spontaneous, too.

The cool rosé wine makes me a little tipsy. I know I'll do whatever He asks me to. I also know He's grateful to me for my gift.

He stares at her, bright-eyed, imagining her breasts under her pale silk shirt. She isn't wearing a bra. She has small breasts and you can make out her hard, dark nipples through the shirt. There's a sprinkling of freckles between her breasts.

She seems very much at ease. I feel very proud of my new "recruit." I can't imagine any of my usual friends here instead of this young foreign model.

She tells them about how we met, but doesn't mention that I kissed Sixtine. She's already realized there are some things that can't be said, and to avoid any misunderstanding, she changes the subject. She tells us about her photo sessions in Ibiza, how the photographer's assistant kept trying to sneak off with her, how her freckles resisted the efforts of the makeup artist. She mentions her house in Formentera.

He puts His hand between my legs and leans toward me and whispers in my ear: "She's magnificent. What a nice gift. Thank you."

I smile at Him. That's the most beautiful compliment He could have given me. The essential thing is that every moment He grants me is a feast for Him. My own unsatisfied desire doesn't matter. All that matters is His pleasure. I'd give Him everything I have, I've even seduced the most beautiful girl I've ever had the luck to meet, just for Him.

Philippe has noticed I have the shoulders of a horsewoman. He rides, too. He says he'd like to ride with me.

I look at Him. He smiles. "If I say so." I'm grateful to Him.

The idea that I'm here to do His bidding excites me and terrifies me. He slips His fingers between my panties and my skin and puckers His lips in what could be a smile. I'm very damp. Ostentatiously, He fondles me a little, then takes out His middle finger and raises it to my mouth. I suck His finger between my lips.

Ingrid and Philippe have been watching every move. Now she lowers her head, but Philippe is still looking at me insistently. I keep His finger between my lips and sustain His friend's gaze.

I want Him to fuck me.

"Let's go," He says at last. He sticks a few bills on the table and drags us after Him.

"Where to?" Ingrid asks.

I'm amused by her boldness. She doesn't know there are some questions He won't answer.

For the first time since He made me His thing, He puts His hand on my shoulder and we walk like that, side by side, along the street.

I interpret the gesture as a sign of affection and find it very moving.

As I walk in the hollow of His shoulder, I observe Ingrid, who's on my left, closely followed by the handsome Philippe.

I can sense she's trying her best to overcome her nervousness.

To encourage her, I put my left arm around her waist.

She smiles at me, and He smiles, too, satisfaction lighting up His dark face.

It's a warm night and the air is mild. We walk as far as the rue du Cherche-Midi, where He takes us through a big metal gate. Ingrid and I look at each other. I find it really amusing to be here in the streets of Paris, at the entrance to a place I've never been, with the most beautiful girl in the world, who's agreed to follow me even though she hardly knows me and certainly has no idea of the nature of the games He likes to subject me to and that are the very reason I've invited her.

I take her hand.

Behind the gate, a succession of dark corridors and shiny steps. At last, we come to a thick black door, padded in leather with brass nails.

He rings. Time passes. Philippe, Ingrid, and I stare at the door. Finally, a peephole opens. An eye must be staring at us, but we can't see it.

I squeeze Ingrid's hand very hard to stop her shaking.

The door opens.

A tall dark man, who looks as if he's come straight from the gym, wearing a Gaultier-style stretch vest cut as low as you can go, puts his head and one shoulder through the door of the unsettling dungeon. His manner isn't very pleasant. All he does is appraise our thin bodies in our loose summer clothes, the colors of which, although very sober—Ingrid in beige and me in gray-blue—seem to surprise him.

"Do you know where you are?"

I find it very hard to contain a laugh of embarrassment and excitement.

If this ill-mannered Cerberus only knew who he was talking to—a supermodel, one of the president's top aides, and two distinguished representatives of the Paris bar!

All He does is nod His head, but His silence speaks volumes.

I observe Philippe, who's hung back a little, maybe one step behind us.

The protein-fed bodybuilder looks us up and down. "You know tonight's a special night?"

Without even parting His thin lips, He smiles, places one hand on Ingrid's shoulder and one hand on mine, and pushes us through the door.

And so we descend, intrigued, into an underworld of depravity.

No sooner have we passed through the cloakroom, where we give false names, than we're struck by the silence and increasing darkness of these cellars.

The walls are mostly tiled, but in some places they're made of thick blocks of eroded stone.

There are some rough areas with chains hanging from them. We're not sure what they're for.

Some thirty slippery steps down, there's a little bar on the right, lit with pink and yellow globes.

The absence of music is surprising. He orders champagne, and I drink my glass in one gulp in order to hide my nervousness from Ingrid. I haven't let go of her hand.

I know she's afraid. It's probably her first time. I suspect she's thinking about her husband and wondering what she's doing here with me and two men she doesn't know.

I give her my most reassuring smile, as if it's up to me to protect her, and spontaneously hug her and raise her hands to my mouth and kiss them.

He moves in close behind me and puts His arms around both of us and kisses me on the mouth. He's surprisingly tender, considering where we are, considering the silence is occasionally shattered by disturbing screams.

He lifts the hem of my dress and touches my shaved cunt with His hand and whispers in my ear: "I'm proud of you." Then He leans over my shoulder and takes Ingrid's tongue between His soft lips. I don't feel any jealousy. All that matters is His pleasure.

I step aside to make His clinch with my friend easier. Philippe has held back so far, but now he joins me without a word and puts his arms around me and tries to kiss me. I turn my head away and give him the kindest smile I can.

"No. I'm His."

Very gently, he opens his hands.

"Don't worry. I won't bother you. I respect you. You're a wonderful girl."

I give him a grateful look. With a nod, He orders me to go. I know He's expecting me to leave Him alone with my friend. Immediately, I take Philippe's hand and suggest we have a look around.

Philippe puts his arm protectively around my shoulder and leads me toward a series of dark alcoves from which we can hear unsettling moans.

We both stop on the threshold of the first alcove, and at once shudder at the sight of a man lying flat on his stomach, his wrists and ankles bound with thin white ropes held in place by what is obviously an extremely tight knot and tied to a pulley fixed to the ceiling. There's a rope around the pulley, held by an exceptionally thin woman, far from young, who seems to be taking great pleasure in pulling jerkily on the rope, which she's coiled around her waist. Although she probably only weighs about a hundred pounds, she manages to lift her lover-cum-playmate, who groans with pain each time she tugs on the rope.

Philippe and I look at each other, puzzled. We're both incredulous, not quite sure what the point of it is.

I'm dying to see Him again but stop myself. I know I'll never know what happened.

Philippe encourages me to continue our visit.

We pass along a corridor full of men walking up and down, apparently in search of an illusory partner. As I pass, they approach me and try to touch me.

Philippe is great, he holds me against him and puts his arms—strong rider's arms—around me. For some reason I can't explain, I trust him and feel reassured in his arms. Occasionally, our eyes meet and we smile at each other, we feel a surprising rapport, here in this place where neither of us belongs.

I don't want him and he respects me. I'm grateful to him for that.

We continue on our way and enter a square vaulted room, its walls shiny with the reflections from a chandelier.

◆ ◆ ◆

At the far end, there's a woman tied to a cross of Saint Andrew. She's hooded and gagged and wearing a tight-fitting latex bodysuit with holes in the chest from which her breasts jut out, swollen by the constricting material.

Each of her nipples is tied to a little chain with a tight slipknot. I remember the time I had to wear something like that.

A number of men are lying on the sticky floor in front of her, licking it. Another man, who's small and round, is beating her thighs as hard as he can with a short whip. Each time the whip, which is weighted with lead, lands with a sharp noise, another pinkish streak appears on her flesh, joining the pattern of crisscrossed lines already there.

I feel a strange trembling at the base of my spine. I'm sorry I can't feel Him behind me right now, when I'm overcome with excitement.

I know He could do anything He wanted with me.

Philippe seems embarrassed. "That's enough of that," he whispers, and we turn back the way we came. I'm infinitely grateful to him.

When we get back to the bar, He's sitting on a stool, and Ingrid is opposite Him, sitting languidly on a squat little armchair. When He sees me, He rises and hugs me. He doesn't ask me for my impressions. He takes me by the hand and leads us all back up the stairs to the mild Parisian night.

No sooner have I arrived at my firm the next day than He calls me on my cell:

"I'm proud of you.

"You were great."

"Philippe's already called me, he thinks you're fantastic. A real bombshell. I told him you weren't a bombshell, but an erupting volcano, and I'm very pleased with you. He asked me for your phone number, but I wouldn't give it to him. I told him I was still keeping you to myself. One day maybe—but not yet.

"See you soon, darling."

Darling. The word sends a shiver through me. I want Him to feel He can't do without me. I want to be part of His life.

XV

I arrive with my husband at my brother's house for what's supposed to be a family dinner, and my heart skips a beat. All my dearest friends are here, my circle of girlfriends who consult me about their love affairs, my companions for fun nights out, overgrown teenagers, my faithful escorts whom I love with a love that will never be anything other than platonic, my riding companions, my favorite colleagues, my three dear sisters and their boyfriends. The champagne flows, the music's lively, it's such a kind, thoughtful gesture, I'm really touched.

Life is extraordinarily carefree and beautiful, I'm infinitely lucky, I know I'm more fulfilled than anybody I know.

◆ ◆ ◆

Inès arrives, too, all smiles, on the arm of her handsome Raphaël. She's impressive in her thigh-length boots and her microskirt above her forty-five-inch legs. Sixtine is here, too, looking very cute in her little turquoise dress. Her cleavage will stay in the memory of many guests for a very long time. Aurélien and Léa throw themselves in my arms, I kiss them, happy they're here, I haven't seen them—out of embarrassment, I suppose—since our evening at the Maison Blanche. Even the famous Arthur has accepted the invitation. He's as handsome as ever. He asks me about the pleasures of Normandy, and I tell him about coal fires and fresh lobster. He tells me he's just broken up with that gorgeous dancer of his, who's thrown herself heart and soul into an outmoded feminism, swapping her bustiers for big eco-friendly leotards, he loved her as he'd rarely loved anyone, but it's all over now, it sputtered and died. My faithful Géraldine is here, smiling at this world she pretends she knows nothing about, because she's chosen to submit to a number of conventions and compromises. Hassan is here, too, we laugh when I tell him he's quite tanned after his holidays—not a compliment he gets very often with his magnificent dark skin.

I think about Him.

I'm not expecting Him. But I'd really like Him to be here, too.

◆ ◆ ◆

I kiss everyone. I'm so touched to see them all together on my birthday. I discover it was my best friend Bérénice who organized everything. Bérénice is more than a dear friend, she's a sister, an ally through thick and thin.

I'm really very touched by so many signs of affection.

Sara tells me she was given the task of inviting my friends from the Bar. I don't dare ask her if she thought of Him. There's no way she could know.

I'm pleased to see my friend the sexy Perrine again. She's much thinner than she was when we last had lunch in the spring, she thanks me for giving her Dr. Strangelove's address and phone number, she's made good use of him, she looks resplendent, and then she quickly tells me about the other great boost she's had in her life: her new Italian boyfriend. My pretty Claire is here, too, my adviser in everything, but more than anything else a brilliant strategist.

The champagne flows and the heat rises, I'm tanned, my hair is long and blond, and I'm looking out for Him, I can't help it.

My sister Justine turns up the volume on the Eastern-style music I'm so fond of. I dance with Bérénice, holding her close, feeling sexy and invulnerable in the middle of all these people I know. Sixtine sways toward us, and Raphaël takes my waist and pulls me away from Bérénice, who laughs and turns back to her fiancé.

A hand grips my shoulder. I don't even have to turn around to know it's Him.

I want Him to kiss me, but He doesn't.

The world stops turning around me, I stop everything to go and get Him a drink and a cigarette and introduce my prettiest friends to Him. As long as they're worthy of me, worthy of Him. If only they knew how I agree to everything provided He's happy, in a world in which all that matters is submission and the giving of yourself, making Him grateful for an evening well spent, a moment well spent, I'd lend them to Him, entrust them to Him, if only He'd take notice of me, too, just a bit, even if it's at the same time, I wouldn't care, just as long as He didn't exclude me, I could prepare them for Him, I'd whisper in their ears and tell them He's so powerful you have to submit to all His demands, I'd tell them He's my God, He's the Devil, He's the absolute fantasy of the lover who comes into your life for a brief moment and then there's nothing, because it'll never be the same again, not after knowing all that, not after knowing Him, you'll never again be able to come like you used to, you'll have to be alone and think about Him and masturbate, because you'll know that sex is more than just foreplay and fucking, that there's the head, too, and that it's so much better with your soul and your mind, with all the strange, mysterious things you don't see coming, which take you by surprise and overwhelm you; I'd like to be able to tell them, I'd like them to know I'm sincere, I'd like them to believe me and to agree to become His playthings, too, obedient little animals who lick and suck and lay themselves open just for His pleasure, because He's the Man, He's my Master.

But I can't tell them: the secret, the bond between us, can't be divulged. First of all, I doubt they'd believe me, and even if they did, they wouldn't understand, desire can't be imagined, only experienced. I'll let Him choose, I'll let Him seduce them, maybe He'll include me in their games, that's all I ask.

The party's really heating up, we're drunk on music and champagne; I keep watching Him secretly, every gesture, every look.

He's already behaving as if He owns the place.

He knows almost nobody, but He's talking to my girl-friends, one after the other, as if they've already submitted to Him, as if He's already conquered them. I'm the only one who knows the devilish hold He has, and I look at all these well-brought-up young girls from good families, married, or about to be married, or looking to be married, still clinging to their adolescent dreams, still searching for their Prince Charming, as they chat innocently to Him without knowing who He is.

We saw too many Walt Disney movies, our mothers didn't warn us, all they talked about was schoolwork and exams and rallies and polo and a sense of honor.

How did I, who not so long ago still felt part of this "caste," get to this point? Why did I follow Him, why did I submit without the least resistance?

My colleague Georges, who I'm more used to seeing in his robes in the Palais de Justice than on the dance floor, maneuvers his way toward me. I look around for Him. With a nod, He tells me to accept this new approach.

With a nonchalance that surprises me, I do as He says. I turn and smile and touch the waist and shoulders of this man I haven't chosen, I sway my hips, languorously, lasciviously, my hair undulates in time with my body, my lips promise wicked kisses. Georges is delighted, he falls in with my dance like a moth attracted by the light, I can feel his hard-on. I smile at Him. With a nod of the head, He congratulates me, urges me to keep going, and takes in between His lips the tongue of a young woman with long black hair who's none other than my oldest school-friend.

Bérénice, who's chanced upon the scene, is throwing me horrified looks. I smile to reassure her and let Georges fondle my hips. But I take care to check where my husband is: he has his back to me, and is deep in a heated discussion with our friend Léon.

Two of my usual knights-errant, who are jealous but haven't grasped the risk they're taking, have approached, in a united front. They try a few moves to get me back, but have to stand there, powerless, and watch the game without knowing the stakes.

They both know Georges means nothing to me, elegant as he may be he doesn't excite me, but they see him embrace me and try to kiss me, they see me turn my mouth away even though my body is swaying in time to his.

Meanwhile, He's already left the young dark-haired woman and turned His attention to Perrine. In a corner of the room, He puts His hands on her opulent breasts. She smiles and takes a step back, I don't know if she's embarrassed or tantalized.

Sixtine joins me, and Georges dances with both of us, and then Sixtine kisses me full on the mouth, as if what I did to her in Saint-Tropez entitled her to be familiar.

◆ ◆ ◆

I look at Him, and He smiles at me. I return Sixtine's kiss
and even hug her, without taking my eyes off Him.

He responds with an encouraging smile. My heart is
beating so hard it feels like it will burst. I can sense He's
proud of me and that's all I ask.

He's already leaving Perrine and joining Léa and her
friend Émilie, who've been sitting comfortably on a corner sofa, talking. As if it were the most natural thing in
the world, they move apart and invite Him to sit down
between them. The three of them laugh. I don't know
what they're telling Him, but his eyes are bright. I'm too
fired up, I can't stand it anymore, I have to hear His voice
and feel His eyes on me, so I walk over to them, deliber-
ately swaying my hips, and sit down at His feet with my
legs folded beneath me, because there isn't an armchair
close enough. He touches my bare shoulder with His forefinger, and I shake all over. Émilie and Léa tell Him how
beautiful they think I am, how desirable they think I am, I
thank them with a smile, they couldn't have given me a
more handsome tribute. He looks at me and agrees. He
tells them He's pleased with me, He's happy to know me,
I'm amazing. I can't get over it, it's a declaration, in front
of witnesses, in front of my friends, I so much want to
kiss Him and bury my nose in His neck and breathe a little of His smell, that smell I'd recognize anywhere, I want

His smell on my clothes and my body, I can barely hold myself back, if He asked me here and now in the middle of all these distinguished, well-behaved people to open my legs, I'd do it, I'd even suck Him right here and now, I close my eyes for a few seconds and imagine His cock, I'd just like to feel Him get a hard-on, feel it inside me at last, at least once, I try to remember the texture of His skin, so soft and so inaccessible here beneath His dark suit and white shirt.

Léa is talking about how she went mad the day I lent her my bustier—the one from Dior, black lace encrusted with little purple roses, which I bought for Him and which He's never seen, never used in His games. Aurélien took her to Rome for the weekend. They'd been out walking late at night and finished up in a rather strange, dimly lit club, full of men and women fondling and fucking. The men were rather old and paunchy, and the women danced to arouse them, giving themselves sometimes to one, sometimes to several. Léa had never seen or experienced anything like it before. Drunk with excitement, she'd found herself getting up on a platform and dancing, too, showing off her statuesque young body to all these strangers. With exaggerated slowness, she'd stripped off her clothes, exhibiting my bustier to all these excited male eyes while Aurélien looked on, amazed. Later, he had brought her back to him, pulled her outside into the

Roman night, and fucked her on the cobblestones of one of those piazzas heavy with history.

He congratulates her warmly and looks at me and I realize He's interested in Léa, too, her story has amused Him, He's excited about the idea of including my young friend in our leisure activities, He wants to deepen the brief acquaintance He had with her that night at the Maison Blanche.

I interpret each of His desires as a promise of pleasure shared, another entry in His diary, one more episode in our story, even though I dread the ending. Can there be a future when there's no hope?

As the party has gone on, a good many of my friends have realized I don't really need them here anymore. My husband has left, too: he has to be up early tomorrow to have breakfast with an important company director.

I'm sitting next to Bérénice, each of us on a chair, opposite Him. He's looking at us, without saying a word. It's quite disturbing, but Bérénice and I brush it aside, we hold hands and look at each other and kiss, so close and so carefree.

Georges returns to the attack, suggesting we go on to

Castel, an old haunt where I earned my first diplomas in seduction.

I decline his invitation with the excuse that I'd rather finish the night at Bérénice's. To show that I'm committed, I kiss her full on the mouth.

He turns on his heels in annoyance and leaves.

Bérénice, He, and I all burst out laughing, which I immediately regret: my suitor has done nothing to deserve such humiliation. I'm a bit angry with myself but immediately forget. The party has narrowed down to a hard core of candidates for initiation: Bérénice, Perrine, and Sixtine. We're watched from a corner by two men in their fifties who are tactfully keeping their distance, accepting the dominance of the inscrutable-looking man who's taken us in hand.

He's sat down on the other side of Bérénice. It's late, and almost all the guests have gone. Even Léa has left, although He tried hard to persuade her to stay.

I can't hold out any longer. I kneel at His feet and kiss His hands. Without saying a word to me, still talking to Bérénice, He strokes my head and presses it gently against His crotch.

I can feel His cock getting harder and my cunt getting wetter.

Perrine and Sixtine are sitting on the floor behind me, with their backs against a sofa, chatting to each other, a full glass of champagne beside them.

He suggests they come closer and join in our conversation, they do as He says without hesitation. I see Him grab Bérénice's hand and invite her to join us at His feet. She, too, complies.

He takes off His black tie and blindfolds Bérénice with it.

"We're going to play blindman's buff.

"You have to identify your friends."

Bérénice looks surprised, but gladly agrees to the game, a game none of us has played for at least twenty years.

As she comes toward us, we laugh and move back.

"Quiet," He reproaches us.

Immediately, we stop giggling and let Bérénice touch us with her outstretched hands.

"Kiss Sixtine," He orders me.

She seems surprised by His peremptory tone but gives me her lips.

Meanwhile, Bérénice has recognized Perrine. He stands up and congratulates her with a kiss on the forehead before removing the blindfold.

Boldly, Sixtine goes up to Him and asks permission to

go and take a pee. I leave the room ahead of her and run down the corridor.

By the time she joins me, I've pulled the body stocking away from my cunt and am pissing copiously, with the door open. Immediately, I give up my place. Sixtine is as drunk as I am but insists that I close the door: she won't be able to do anything if I'm watching. We both laugh uproariously. After a lot of teasing, I finally agree to close the door.

At the same moment, I hear His steps behind me, He pushes me flat against the wall and immediately plunges his fingers into my cunt. I turn and kiss Him. Kiss Him and kiss Him, hug Him with all my might. His tongue is hot and gentle, I feel good, I want him so much I could die, I don't care about the others in the drawing room, or Sixtine behind the door.

I search greedily for His cock inside his trousers. I extricate it without difficulty. It's very hard. I take it in my mouth. He stands with His back against the wall and opens His legs and grabs my hair, while my lips move back and forth and I lick Him with my tongue, savoring every fraction of an inch He's consenting to give me of Himself.

I've forgotten Sixtine, and jump when I hear the toilet door opening. I lift my head and see Him grab her by the shoul-

ders and sink His tongue into her mouth. He puts His
hands on her breasts and reaches inside her dress to pull
them out and sucks and bites her nipples. I know that pain,
I envy her. I take Him in my mouth again and close my eyes
to concentrate on His pleasure. He's grabbed my hair in a
firm grip, keeping my head in place, and I apply myself to
sucking and licking this adulated cock, taking it deep into
my throat, while with one hand I fondle and knead all His
sensitive parts. Blinded by the dark, soft, curly hairs of His
lower belly, I give up trying to keep track of all the nice
things He's doing to my friend, although the moans I hear
make it clear how aroused she is.

I'd like to make Him come right now, but despite all
the zeal I'm devoting to His taut cock He remains totally
in control.

Now He pulls on my hair and lifts me up and, with His
hands still in Sixtine's cunt, turns His lips away from her
mouth to take mine.

I respond to His kiss with a violence and excitement to
match my emotion. I want Him all to myself. But He immediately takes His lips away from me and, still holding my hair
tight, moves my face toward Sixtine's and presses my mouth
to hers. Her lips open and her teeth bite me a little, but finally
she succumbs and the combination of my kisses and His
hands burrowing into her cunt unleashes a series of intense
moans. Without waiting for His orders, I take the initiative

and tease her hard pink nipples between my fingers and knead her heavy breasts, which are so big I can't hold them in my hands. I press myself against Him, my legs apart, my back arched in an exaggerated fashion, I want Him inside me so much, no matter which way He enters, I could scream. I free one of my hands and take hold of His cock, in the hope of drawing it inside me, but He pushes me away and shifts His body until He's behind Sixtine. Her cry as He penetrates her, and the way her upper body tips toward me, make it clear He's sodomizing her, and the gut-wrenching pain I feel seems to me much worse than all the blows and all the mistreatment He's inflicted on me so far. To hide the sadness that's over-whelming me, I close my eyes and kneel in front of her and start to suck her clitoris—she's making a lot of noise, the thrusts of His cock are tearing her apart, and with each thrust she cries out, and each cry is like the lash of a whip biting into my flesh, and my tears fall as she comes, violently, leaning on me, her nails digging into my shoulders, and when I take my lips away from her fulfilled clitoris and look up, I see Him throw His head back and grimace and screw up His eyes as He relieves Himself, with obvious relish, in my friend's ass.

But why her? I feel sick. Much sicker than she does.

We go back and join the others. Tactfully, they pretend they haven't noticed anything. They're sitting on the sofas,

calmly continuing with the business of getting drunk. One
of the boys lights a huge joint and hands it to me with a
smile. I take two long, deep drags and sit down next to
Him on the sofa. He takes my hand and pulls me to Him.
I snuggle against His shoulder.

Bérénice flicks between Johnny and Jane Birkin. I'm moved
by the song "Que je t'aime," and my eyes fill with tears.

Maybe He senses it, or maybe He himself is moved for a
moment, because He hugs me very tight. I'm so happy, I
could cry out. I hug Him back, and He kisses me, very
tenderly. His lips are soft and His tongue voluptuous. I
needed this kiss so much, I abandon myself to it completely and, without realizing where I am, or what I'm
doing, sit down astride Him to be in a better position to
put my arms around Him. He's very gentle and very tender, and I place my head in the hollow of His neck and
stroke His face. He plays with my hair and strokes my
bare shoulders and runs His hands up my legs and
moves the body stocking aside and very gently rubs my
cunt.

His face is against mine.
"I'm proud of you," He whispers. "You're great. You're
much better than anyone else I've trained so far. This is

your birthday and you've given me a really nice present, a really pleasant surprise. I'm proud of you."

I close my eyes and hold Him very tight.

I'm haunted by the image of His cock penetrating Sixtine. I go to sleep with her cries in my head, and wake up in tears, seeing again His grimace as He came inside her.

Why not me? Why won't He fuck me? For months I've been thinking maybe He couldn't, but the violent way I saw Him and felt Him fuck Sixtine tells me I was wrong.

The pain just won't go away.

I'm in my office and I feel tears rolling down my cheeks. I don't understand it. I don't understand Him. On the one hand, I feel as if we've built up a real relationship, He seems closer, gentler, more attentive. On the other hand, looking at it objectively, I have to admit He doesn't give me anything, anything, at all, He won't even lower Himself to fuck me. How can I feel so dependent on Him when He won't even touch me? The power of the mind terrifies me. I feel as if I really belong to Him.

XVI

I've never told anybody about our little evening with Ingrid and Philippe. I've never discovered if anything happened between Him and Ingrid. When she and I had lunch together shortly afterward, I carefully avoided the subject. I don't see what useful purpose would be served by knowing.

Ingrid phones me at my office to invite us (Him and me) for a weekend in her beloved house in Formentera.

I leap at the suggestion. The idea of Him and me forming "a couple," for however short a time, seems like a unique opportunity to make myself just that little bit more useful, more necessary, more enticing to Him.

◆ ◆ ◆

Ingrid says she's never said anything to Godefroy about our little four-way dinner in August, but she has told her husband a lot about me, and ever since he's been teasing her endlessly about introducing me to him.

The day He deigns to send for me, in between giving Him a few daring caresses, I tell Him about my new friend's invitation. He accepts without the slightest hesitation, and I devote the days before our departure to getting ready for this secret escapade.

Although Ingrid has told me all I need to take is a pair of jeans and a couple of swimsuits, I stuff my bag full of fine lingerie and dresses with low necklines and transparent sarongs, and borrow Bérénice's Gucci sandals, which are a good four-plus inches high—unless Ingrid is wearing Tod's, there'll only be less than an inch between us.

On His orders, I go to Erès and buy a black tulle garter belt and matching designer stockings for Ingrid. I wish I had them, too. What I'd like more than anything is for Him to give me a gift one day. A real gift, something He chose, something that cost Him money. At least that would prove He cared about me a little.

I know we're all very keyed up, anticipating a weekend of debauchery.

◆ ◆ ◆

His perversity intrigues me, and His kindness worries me. A few days before we leave, I tell Him about the recurrent nightmares I've been having lately, nightmares in which He orders me to let *another man* fuck me. Strange as it may seem, after all the months of strict training and all the mistreatment, there's still a line I won't cross: I can't bear the thought of another man's cock inside me, that's one humiliation that is too horrible to bear, I could fuck all the girls He wanted, prepare each of my friends one after the other and then give them to Him, I'd agree to seduce their boyfriends in exchange, but being penetrated by a third party completely turns me off. All I want is HIM. And despite the fact that He won't touch me, I'm absolutely faithful to Him. I know His feelings, or rather His lack of feelings, for me don't allow for jealousy, but I don't want Him to give me away. The only order I couldn't possibly carry out, the only order I'd have to disobey if I didn't want to plunge into a deep depression, would be to place my body at the disposal of other men's cocks. He knows that and plays on it.

I want Him more than anything else. I need to feel Him inside me.

◆ ◆ ◆

I've never been tempted by casual sex with strangers or one-night stands, and I feel nothing but disgust at the prospect of being fucked by another man.

I want Him.

Several times, sensing my hesitation in obeying His orders, He's kept me in line by threatening to subject me to a gang bang. He'd force me with blows and insults to get down naked on all fours like a bitch and offer my vaginal and anal orifices to all these other men with their hard, eager cocks. Rough hands would grab my hips, unknown cocks would transfix me, I'd scream but He'd hit my face with His long, tapering hand and pull my hair back and lift my head and slap me again; He'd press His foot on my lower back and make me arch like a real slut and all the men would insult me in turn before they fucked me, poor souls alleviating their sense of inferiority, at least for the time it takes them to ejaculate, with the incredible sensation of humiliating and fucking a bourgeois woman, and gaining a feeling of domination from it—an illusory feeling, since I belong only to my Master, who's chosen, I suppose out of some desire for recognition, to offer them the woman who's given herself to Him.

◆ ◆ ◆

One Wednesday afternoon full of sunshine and the joys of spring, after I've told Him about this recurring nightmare, He sends for me, and kisses me and licks me and sodomizes me with His fingers, and whispers in my ear that I'm His best pupil and He'll take care of me.

I don't really know what to make of that, but by the time I leave, I feel a bit calmer, convinced that He cares enough about me to keep His promises. I trust Him.

The wind is blowing really hard as we get off the plane. Godefroy has ordered a taxi, and it's waiting for us outside the terminal, to drop us at the boat that will take us to Formentera.

I see Him in a new light. He leaps like a young goat when He sees the choppy sea, takes deep breaths, looks up at the Mediterranean sky, and smiles. I've forgotten He spent His childhood by the sea, though not this one.

Ingrid's so sweet to me, she knows how tense I am in anticipation of this weekend, which I'll surely never live through again. She knows I'm aware how unreal the coming hours will be, because one day, in a month or a year or maybe even tomorrow, He'll leave my life as He entered it, His desire will either be dead or be aroused by some other creature He'll feel the need to test His power of domination on. Never for a moment has it occurred to me that I could be the one who decides to stop, to put an end to the way my heart quivers as soon as I think about Him, as soon as I hear His voice, as soon as I feel His skin or smell His smell.

Formentera is an incredible island, so natural, so amazingly unspoiled for such a built-up part of the Mediterranean, the big church square is so authentic, empty except for a few fresh produce shops, people walk around in jeans and beige sweaters, but we're not on the Île de Ré or any other off-shoot of France.

When we get to our hosts' house, we find a tray of oysters waiting for us on the doorstep.

I'm very touched by Ingrid's thoughtfulness: she's remembered I told her He loves oysters.

I watch Him out of the corner of my eye. He's brimming over with happiness. I've never before seen Him really smile, never heard Him laugh.

No sooner have we gotten inside the house than He asks Godefroy where our rooms are—they're upstairs—and hurries to take our bags up, drops them inside the room, and takes me in His arms and hugs me very tight and asks

me to give Ingrid her gift and convince her that we should
change for dinner.

I take a deep breath. I realize the dance is about to begin.
I take the little package from Erès out of my travel bag
and give it to Ingrid.

"You know the kind of images we're going to leave in
His head matter a lot to Him. I think it's time we submitted to the dress code."

Ingrid smiles and takes the package, but I know her
well enough by now to know that although she looks
relaxed, there's an anxiety there that she isn't sure she can
keep under control.

Seeing the four little clips on the garter belt, she bursts
out laughing.

"But what is this thing?"

"You're going to be very, very beautiful. Come on, I'll
help you put it on," and I take her hand and lead her into
the bathroom, where we shut ourselves in.

In no time at all, she's taken her clothes off. Naked, her
tall, willowy body is even more spectacular than I imagined. I congratulate her, tell her I think she's really magnificent, and kiss her lightly on the cheek. Then I slip the
garter belt around her hips and stretch the designer stockings over her endless legs.

"I can't go downstairs like this."

I agree. Unable to stop giggling, she shows me her wardrobe, and we finally opt for a little black silk dress, which is so short the tops of her stockings are still visible.

"What about you?"

"Oh, I've come equipped."

She helps me with the hooks of my famous Dior bustier with the purple roses—the one I lent Léa for her weekend in Rome—and watches me with a smile as I put on my black crossover dress and my stockings and my shoes with their exaggeratedly high heels.

"Well?" we hear from downstairs.

Clearly, the boys are getting impatient.

I push her toward the stairs, and the two of us walk down, giggling like two little girls who've dressed up as femmes fatales but don't take their roles at all seriously.

He's been waiting for us, sitting comfortably with His legs crossed on an old fawn leather sofa, His shirt slightly open, His eyes bright. Godefroy is standing a bit farther back, a glass of champagne in his hand. This is the first chance I've had to get a good look at him. Although he's much older than Ingrid, there's something unusually ele-gant in the way he moves, the way he conducts himself, something proud about the way he holds his head. He's slightly balding and he wears his salt-and-pepper hair in curls on the back of his neck. His eyes sparkle with intelligence and I sense he's someone who's curious about life and full of enthusiasm.

Ingrid skips up to him, twirling her dress as she does so, happy to give him a glimpse of her underwear. With rather more restraint, I go and stand in front of Him, my legs a little apart, my back arched.

Instinctively, I put my hands together behind my back.

Ingrid has sat down next to her husband, and both of them are watching us. Slowly, with an action that reminds me of the first time He sent for me, He runs His hand over my ankles and up my legs, lifting the back of my dress a little as He does so.

When He reaches my crotch, He moves the panties aside and touches my cunt. I close my eyes, concentrating on the sensation.

He stops before I come. I open my eyes again and kneel to kiss Him, but He indicates with a flick of His eyes that He prefers me to stand. I immediately do as He says. He unfastens the belt of my dress and slips it over my shoulders. It falls to the floor, spreading out over the earthenware tiles.

I'm standing in the middle of the living room, in my elegant bustier, my back exaggeratedly arched.

♦ ♦ ♦

With a sideways glance, I see that Ingrid and Godefroy have stopped kissing and are watching us.

"Is she beautiful? Do you like her?" He asks, without taking His eyes off me.

"Stunning," says Ingrid while Godefroy stares at me like an expert sizing up a horse.

"I'll lend her to you. You can do what you like with her."

He stands up and goes to join them. I stay in the middle of the room, not daring to move.

Now Ingrid stands up and comes to me and kisses me. "Darling, you're magnificent," she says, in her charming accent.

I return her kisses, glad she's taken it on herself to look after me.

There follows a kind of dance between the two of us. The two men, of course, don't miss a second of it.

Ingrid clasps me to her sublime body and moves her mouth lightly over my face and the back of my neck and my bare shoulders. I set off to discover her skin, her breasts, the hollows of her body. I linger on her freckles, kissing them and moving my finger over them. We embrace and fondle, trying with our fingers, our mouths, our lips, to arouse the most sensitive points of each other's body.

Godefroy has come up to us. I tremble when he places his hand on my thighs. He moves his fingers over my face and around my eyes and onto my lips, and I turn and kiss him.

I feel His eyes on me, watching me. When my tongue meets Godefroy's, He smiles.

When He takes Ingrid in His arms, she turns to me, like a true friend, looking for my approval before she responds. I give it with a smile, and then close my eyes and try hard not to think about anything.

He's touching her. I can hear her breathing, I want to be in her place. Godefroy, getting bolder, inserts his middle finger between my legs.

Ingrid pushes Him away gently and comes back to her husband, who immediately turns and takes her in his arms.

She takes off her dress. She's naked now apart from the garter belt and the stockings, which accentuate the perfection of her body.

Godefroy sits down on the sofa, and she sits down on top of him. They barely move. From the expression in her eyes, I guess that all she's doing is contracting her vagina around his cock. The pleasure I can see on his face tells me I'm right.

◆ ◆ ◆

I want Him. I kneel at His feet and move closer to the bulge I see rising in front of me. Very gently, I slide my lips around His cock and begin sucking on it, with slow, regular movements. From time to time, I withdraw my mouth and lick underneath, with little flicks of my tongue, back and forth, but try as I might, I can't reach His anus. So instead I put my left forefinger inside, sliding it in as far as I can and turning it, while I continue moving my whole mouth up and down His cock. I concentrate, focusing on His pleasure, which I can feel mounting, aware of every particle of skin my tongue comes in contact with. I sense Godefroy kneeling behind me to fondle me while Ingrid kisses him. I push him away when he tries to enter me. He doesn't insist, but gets back on his feet and returns to Ingrid and plunges into her again from behind, still standing—she has opened her long legs wide to make it easier for him.

Now He takes me by the shoulders and pulls me up and sits down on the sofa.

I hug Him as tight as I can and beg Him to fuck me, here and now, finally, I can't go on like this, it's been too long, I want to feel Him inside me, I can't wait any longer, all these months, all this desire, I kneel by Him, His hands in mine, and look in His eyes and beg Him. He smiles but doesn't answer.

◆ ◆ ◆

Godefroy and Ingrid leave the room, their steps on the stairs tell me they're heading for the shelter of their bedroom.

Not long after, He takes me by the hand and leads me up to "our" bed. They've left the door of their room open, and I catch a glimpse of them making love very tenderly. He's lying on top of her, and she's moaning languorously.

I'm quite intimidated at the thought of sleeping by His side. It's the first time we're going to be in a bed together, and I'm more scared of this intimacy than of anything He's yet asked of me.

He gets into bed first, naked. I put on one of those vintage negligees with thin straps that I collect, and join Him. He takes me in His arms. When I'm lying on my back, He raises Himself on one elbow and kisses me. When I open my lips to receive His tongue, He takes His mouth away and puts it back again with infinite gentleness. I surrender to this kiss and my senses explode. I detect a tenderness He's never shown me before, and that I'd never have suspected.

He spends a long time like this kissing me. He's on top of me. I feel the weight of His body. The sweetness and warmth of His mouth are intoxicating. With one hand He strokes my breasts and my stomach and then moves it inside me. With extraordinary dexterity, He increases the pressure of His fingers. I feel as if I'm about to come. I take His hand in mine and draw it out of me.

I beg Him to fuck me.

He kisses me again on the lips.

I beg Him to fuck me.

He kisses my cunt.

I beg Him to fuck me.

He makes me cry out.

And then NOTHING.

Later, much later, I fall asleep, curled up in the hollow of His body. I'm happy and I want to cry.

Even later, I dream about His cock forcing its way into my anus, I put my hand between my legs to alleviate the pain, which is gradually becoming pleasurable. Our almost simultaneous orgasm floods my sleep with light.

I take His hand, which is resting on my body, and squeeze it. I grip His fingers and tears roll down my cheeks. I want Him too much. Why won't He fuck me?

The emotion is extreme, a kind of overwhelming despair. It's more intense than anything I've ever felt before. The meaning of passion. The violence of desire. The senselessness of frustration.

I wake up in the early hours, my head heavy. My pillow is wet with my silent tears.

It's an incredibly hot September morning.

As He wolfs down a croissant, He gets excited by Godefroy's suggestion that we spend the day on his boat. Ingrid and I set off to buy Parma ham, figs, and melons for a picnic on board.

Formentera is bathed in a soft light. We pass a group of Italians who are talking loudly, and who turn to look at us.

Ingrid asks me how my night was. She congratulates me on our discretion, she didn't hear a thing despite the thinness of the walls.

I lie, and tell her I fell asleep very quickly, I'd been really exhausted and the sea air knocked me out. I wipe my eyes discreetly. I can't tell her He refuses to fuck me. She wouldn't understand. Nobody would understand. I feel alone. I think about my son and my husband and about my life, which I'm jeopardizing for an affair that isn't an affair.

On my ridiculously high Guccis, it's a bit difficult to follow Him. But at least I know I look good, with my tanned legs and my arched back and my new black Erès top and matching muslin sarong, which I've tied, as short as I can, around my hips. Godefroy is carrying the picnic basket. I look at the people we pass and wonder if they have any inkling, if their lives are anything like ours.

Our hosts' little powerboat is very comfortable, the foredeck is covered with huge mattresses.

◆ ◆ ◆

Ingrid, Godefroy, and He are in an extremely good mood, laughing as if they had grown up together and share the same secrets.

No sooner has the boat left port than Ingrid drags me fore and suggests I strip off my clothes. "At least here we can sunbathe without getting any marks," she says, slipping out of her bathing suit.

The motor hums and gains speed. The coast is magnificent, spectacular, wild.

Ingrid asks me to oil her back. I massage her from the neck down to just above the buttocks.

The boat soon stops in a small cave. The walls of rock surrounding it are the color of saffron in the Mediterranean light. Ingrid rushes to the prow and, on the pretext of telling Godefroy the best moment to drop anchor, leans over to look down at the bottom of the sea.

The fleeting image of that incredible girl, stretching her legs and jutting her body forward, will remain engraved on everyone's memory. No sooner has the anchor sunk in the underwater sands and Ingrid stood back up again than we hear the sound of someone diving into the transparent water. When I go to the aft deck a few minutes later, I see Him, naked under the water, His muscles rippling as He swims the breaststroke.

Godefroy leaves the controls and joins Him. I suggest to Ingrid that we put together a platter of food, topped off with cherry tomatoes and served with rosé wine. She agrees, though she pokes gentle fun at the way I'm always trying to do my best for Him, always carrying out His orders before He's even given them, and we hurry belowdecks and come back out again a few minutes later, our arms loaded with refreshments.

Now Ingrid dives in, and with a graceful crawl soon reaches the boys, who are swimming toward the coast, in search of sea urchins, I suppose.

The three naked bodies glide noiselessly through the water. The only sound is the seagulls squawking above our boat, no doubt in expectation of the leftovers from our picnic.

I watch the gulls and think about the son I've abandoned for a whole weekend and the lies I've told my husband and the values my parents tried to instill in me. And I see myself here on the deck of a boat, in a Spanish cove I'm not supposed to know about, with a couple who aren't really my friends, trying to please a man who gives me nothing in return, who doesn't love me, doesn't respect me, and keeps me in an inexplicable state of dependence I can't escape.

◆ ◆ ◆

I think again about the terrible prediction I was given. *One day, a woman will be killed.* I'm afraid. I feel as if I'm no longer in control of myself.

I fear for my life.

Voices float up from the ocean, inviting me to join them. I have no desire to dive in, I don't like swimming.

They soon emerge from the sea one by one. But He immediately balances on the aft deck and jumps in again with a spectacular and dangerous dive. For a moment, I imagine His childhood by the sea, see Him running on the beach, having His first sexual experiences in the sand.

Ingrid takes a shower. Godefroy kisses her while the water is still running down her body. I serve the glasses of cool rosé.

He's sat down beside me and put His arm around my shoulders. It's a surprising thing to do, but everything becomes clear when He leans toward me and whispers a command in my ear. He wants me to "look after" Godefroy, who's sitting calmly opposite us.

I squeeze His hand to give myself at least a shred of courage and get up and go and stand in front of Godefroy.

I look at Ingrid, who gives me her permission. I lean down and kiss him.

My friend's husband seems quite pleased with my initiative and responds to my kiss by inserting his hand in my bikini bottom—the only thing I'm wearing—and moving it away, to get at the inside of my cunt. I feel His eyes on me and let him do it. "You're very wet," is all he says, putting his moistened finger in his mouth. His cock makes a bulge in his swimsuit.

As for Him, He's stood up and approached Ingrid and is fondling her pointed breasts. She sighs and gives Him her lips, which He immediately takes.

For a moment, we look at each other. I can see His desire for her in His eyes and I know what's going to happen.

He strokes her chest and shoulders and moves His hands down to her buttocks. They're both the same height, and they stand there, straining toward each other as if their stomachs are joined by a magnet. He touches her cunt, then crouches to lick her. She opens her legs to let His tongue enter more freely, and her hands grip the guardrail of the boat.

At the sight of his wife yielding, Godefroy pushes his fingers farther into me and begins moving them back and forth between my cunt and my ass.

◆ ◆ ◆

I'm afraid he wants to fuck me and I turn away from him
and go to Him. Looking for a distraction, I kiss Ingrid on
the lips, then take her breasts in my mouth. They're as hard
as green apples. But He stands up and asks me to go back
to Godefroy. I know He wants me to leave Ingrid to Him.

I think again of the club in the rue du Cherche-Midi where
I'd let myself be dragged away by Philippe, leaving Ingrid to
Him. I've never found out what happened. I've never
wanted to know. It's better if I never know.

But today I don't think I could bear the sight of Him pos-
sessing this woman in front of me. I'm haunted by the
images of last night, His persistent refusal to fuck me.

Why is He so determined to keep His pleasure distinct
from mine? Why won't He come inside me at the same
time as He makes me come? I want Him. I want Him
between my legs, between my buttocks, I want Him to
take possession of me with His cock, I want Him to cry
out when He's deep inside me.

Daring to defy His repeated instructions, I don't let go of
Ingrid. I kneel and take her open cunt between my lips
and suck her juices—they're a bit acidic, she's quite damp

inside—and put in two of my fingers and rub the wall in front of her vagina with one of them and turn the other one slightly, trying to push in as far as it'll go, and put my other hand into her anus and move in and out to the rhythm of her moans, though maybe it's my own movements that are causing them. Meanwhile, I keep moving my tongue around her clitoris, sucking it tenderly, licking it. With two fingers buried in her cunt, which oozes moisture as her pleasure mounts, I plunge the whole of my middle finger into her anus and turn it, trying to part the walls, feeling her sphincter tightening and relaxing.

He has slipped behind Ingrid and pushes away my hand and replaces it with His own. I'm at the same height as His huge cock, and take the opportunity to masturbate Him.

Suddenly I feel Godefroy, who's knelt behind me and is pushing himself against me, ready to enter me. I stiffen, and take my mouth away from between Ingrid's legs.

I grab His wrist and squeeze it tightly. It's like a cry for help. But He tugs on my hair and brings my mouth back to Ingrid's cunt, which closes around me, demanding me.

He orders me to give in.

His voice is unequivocal, there's no point in arguing. I

tremble and hold on to His hand, screaming silently, begging Him not to give me to this man I don't want, this man who isn't Him.

He puts His mouth against my ear and whispers that I'm His, I have to obey Him, I'm a good pupil, a nice girl who wants to please her Master.

I close my eyes and try not to think.

I know it's too late. The image of my son flashes through my mind. I think about my lies, I think about my husband.

Godefroy plunges into me.

My nails dig into His fingers.

He knows. He's known all along that all I wanted is Him.

And He watches me being fucked by a man I don't want.

My legs won't carry me anymore, I'm shaking, my eyes fill with tears.

He still has my hair in a tight grip but, aware no doubt of my distress, moves my face toward Him and kisses me.

◆ ◆ ◆

I feel as if I'm someone else. I'm outside my own body and I no longer feel the thrusts of the cock inside me.

His kiss means nothing to me.

As if I were dead, I watch Him as He takes His mouth away from mine and stands up and starts to fuck the beautiful Ingrid, who welcomes Him with a voluptuous sigh.

Her body writhes with pleasure.

He takes firm hold of her hips.

I don't want to think. I don't want to think about anything. I don't want to see Him plunging His cock into her as He's never done to me, fucking her as He's never deigned to fuck me, responding to her pleas as He's never responded to mine. And there she is, in front of me, my friend, in front of me, with His cock inside her, and Him thrusting against her buttocks, squeezing her hips with His hands, fucking her.

My eyes mist over as Godefroy moves in and out, his head thrown back, his eyes closed in pleasure.

Now He withdraws with a groan, and as if He's given the signal for a break, Godefroy lets go of me, too. The two men serve themselves two more glasses of rosé. They're radiant with contentment.

He hugs me very tight and kisses me fiercely. I try to abandon myself to His kiss, try to chase away this overwhelming feeling of sadness.

He tells me He's very proud of me, I constantly surprise Him, surpass all His expectations. He's suddenly very gentle and very tender.

I don't care.

I'd like to erase what happened from my memory.

Later, when the sun has gone and the air has grown cooler, I jump down from the boat in an advanced state of exhaustion. I feel completely drained, I feel as if my legs have been cut from under me.

But I still manage to walk across the harbor with dignity, stepping carefully on my high-heeled sandals. People look at my dark figure. We don't say a word to one another, I suppose we're all sated after such an intoxicating day, a day that will mark us forever.

◆ ◆ ◆

By the time we reach the house, I'm not feeling very well. I take a can of Diet Coke from the fridge and go up to my room and collapse on the bed, my body still completely salted and sanded and soiled.

He stays downstairs. I hear His voice and the voices of the others.

I close my eyes and think about my baby. I try to convince myself that you have to take responsibility for your actions, and that I chose life, adventure, passion.

But it hurts. It hurts all over.
  I cry.

I don't know if it's my own sadness, or the atmosphere of the evening, but none of us is very talkative. The excitement has subsided.

  I suppose we've all given too much of ourselves, and need to find ourselves again. Ingrid is very close to Godefroy, she's so tender toward him, so gentle. I look at them and envy them. They talk about their plans for a child, and can't stop hugging and kissing.

I feel alone.

◆ ◆ ◆

He doesn't speak to me, doesn't even look at me. The boys have decided to go out for dinner, and I feel ridiculous in my elegant bustier and my high heels, which for the first time seem out of place. I'd like to lose myself in the folds of a big djellaba. I'd like to be alone, I'd like to see my son and my husband again. I'd like to call them and tell them how much I love them. I can't. My husband thinks I'm at a friend's house in Brittany, and he might ask me for the phone number.

Godefroy orders tapas for everyone. I feel strange. I'm not at all well. I don't want to eat.

I don't talk, and barely listen to them. I don't even know what they're talking about. Anyway, He doesn't say a word to me.

I'd like to be in my house in Normandy, on my big blue sofa, reading stories to my son.

No sooner have we gotten back to the house than Godefroy and Ingrid go up to their room. They hold hands as they climb the stairs.

He sits down in an armchair and starts watching a stupid variety show.

◆ ◆ ◆

I'd so much like to have His arms around me but He doesn't
so much as glance at me, just sits there in His armchair, alone.

Sometime later, He calls my name and asks me to pour
Him a glass of cognac. When I return with the glass in my
hand, He gestures to me to kneel and unbuttons His jeans
and gives me His cock, which isn't erect.

I take it in my mouth while it's still soft and apply
myself to reviving it. He sips His drink without taking His
eyes off the television.

A little later, I climb the stairs with a bitter taste in my
mouth and go to bed, alone.

I wake up in the night and notice He's lying a long way
from me in this extramarital bed. It takes me a long time
to get back to sleep, my eyes misty with distress.

The daylight is streaming in through the blinds. I watch
Him sleeping, His face half buried in the pillow. My eyes
follow the line of His shadow on the white sheet, as if
tracing it with my finger.

◆ ◆ ◆

His features are so fine, they could be a woman's. His eyes are closed, there are occasional little tremors under His eyelids, and when that happens, His surprisingly thin lips close and seem to emit a slight sucking sound.

In sleep, He seems so gentle. A strange feeling of peace comes from this man I know is the Devil.

His long, nimble fingers grip the sheet covering our bodies.

Silence reigns within these walls, mute witnesses of our debauchery.

He opens His eyes, stretches and yawns and blinks. He seems completely unaware of my presence. He hasn't touched me all night.

I don't want Him to see my face first thing in the morning, so I bury my head in the pillow, and turn my back to Him. If He wanted, He could seize my skin in His teeth, like a wild beast hungry for fresh white flesh.

But He doesn't, instead He turns around and, in a voice completely devoid of humor that leaves me absolutely stunned, orders me to get dressed immediately and go out to buy croissants, plain and chocolate, and fresh oranges, which I'll have to squeeze myself, and the Sunday newspaper.

I can't believe my ears. I don't know what to say. I'm so stunned, I just get up without a word and set off for the village, which is still asleep.

By the time I get back twenty minutes later, my arms loaded with food, Ingrid and Godefroy are up. They're delighted by the warm croissants. They make coffee. Godefroy gives me an affectionate hug and asks me if I had a good night. I answer something polite but meaningless. Just as Ingrid is putting the steaming coffeepot on the table, He comes down.

We sit for a long time over our coffee and croissants. I don't say a word as He talks about Helen, the woman He loves and shares His life with: how she rushes out every morning while He's still asleep to buy Him croissants and newspapers and comes back and puts a white tablecloth and fresh roses on the breakfast table and makes Him burning hot coffee and watches Him eat and makes sure He doesn't need anything and keeps quiet so that she can listen to Him talk, and how she perfumes with flower essences the entrance to the building and the eighty-three steps He'll climb to the door of their apartment and how she arranges dozens of tiny candles along a path that leads Him to a big hot bath scented with essential oils and strewn with rose petals, and how she's

taken classes with Lenôtre so that every night, whether
He's going to be in or not, she can cook Him a feast worthy of a great chef, and how she packs His bags for Him
when He goes away and has thought of everything for
this weekend.

Ingrid throws me a dismayed, sympathetic glance, but I
feel nothing.

It's weird how cold and empty I feel, as if I've been anes-
thetized.
    He talks about Helen and I don't care, I hear His words
but I don't really listen.

When He claps His hands and tells me to clear the table, I
stand up and do as He says, as if it's of no importance.

Godefroy goes with me, symbolically picking up his own
empty cup.

In the kitchen, he puts his arms around my shoulders and
embraces me. I let him do it but my obvious lack of enthusiasm stops him in his tracks.
    "I'm not feeling too inspired this morning," I say sim-
ply, and take his hands away.

◆ ◆ ◆

By the time we rejoin Ingrid and Him in the garden, He's kneeling in front of her and she's opening her long legs as wide as she can.

I'm suddenly overcome with nausea.

Godefroy, who's been walking behind me, tries to put his hands between my legs.

Unconcerned, I let him do it. But when I feel his stomach against my lower back, I turn quickly and tell him I had a bad night and feel really tired, and slip away.

I take the stairs four at a time and close the bedroom door and dive into bed.

I think with all my might about my baby. I don't know what I'm doing here anymore.

Sometime later, I'm not sure how long, as I lie huddled between the sheets, I hear the door being flung open.

His voice is harsher than I've ever known it.

"What's all this playacting?"

I can't answer. My eyes are filling with tears.

"Are you making fun of me? I don't like tantrums."

" . . ."

"Answer me! I can't stand this childishness! I warn you, there's no way I'm going to let you make a scene, do you understand? Do you want me to lose my temper?"

He grips my shoulder violently and shakes it, then raises His hand and brings it down as hard as He can on my face, which I try to hide under the sheets.

But I get my breath back.

"That's enough!" I say in a low voice. "I don't want to play your games anymore! I can't! I'm not making a scene, I'll never make a scene, it's just that I can't go on, it's too hard."

He showers me with blows. I weep silently and stare at His hands as they rise in the air and come crashing down on me.

By the time He stops, my face hurts, especially my upper lip, which feels swollen and particularly painful. Blood mingles with my saliva. I sit up and look Him in the eyes.

"I've worshiped you like a god. But I can't play this game anymore. It's over. It's too hard for me. I can't go on."

In all these long months, I've never ever imagined I wouldn't be able to obey Him. But now I'm telling the truth. I can't go on.

◆ ◆ ◆

I look at Him. He catches His breath, and for the first time seems bewildered, thrown off balance.

"Very well. *Point taken.* But listen to me. What you've experienced with me, you'll never experience again. Nobody will ever treat you as I've treated you. You'll never again have an orgasm without thinking of this, without thinking of me."

I smile. His vanity suddenly seems ridiculous.

"In three hours," He goes on, emphasizing His words, "we'll leave this house. You'll go, back to your girl-friends, your daily routine, your little well organized bourgeois life. Until then, you have to do exactly what I ask of you."

And He launches into a speech about how I owe it to Ingrid, for the sake of her peace of mind, her marriage, not to spoil this weekend, not to jeopardize her life and the children she wants with her husband.

The point of it all is that it's vital that I give my hosts everything they want, and in particular devote the few remaining hours to Godefroy's pleasure. He's so thoughtful toward a couple He hardly knows.

◆ ◆ ◆

I feel drunk and tired. Broken. Betrayed.

I promise to do as He says. And I keep my word.

———◆———

I've never heard from Him again. His number has never again flashed up. He's never sent for me again.

I've never felt His cock inside me. I've never known what He thought of me.

Pain. The insistent pain of having lost everything. Even my trust. In myself. In men. Thinking I'm nothing but a cunt and a mouth, available, trained, perfect. Perfect. Perfect for men's pleasure. So well trained. Unworthy to receive. Unworthy of recognition, unworthy of love. Repeating that I'm worth nothing. Nothing. I was only a plaything in His hands.

Because I loved a man who didn't love me. Because I gave everything to a man who didn't even see me. Because I did everything and received NOTHING.

EMPTINESS.

◆ ◆ ◆

Tears. As soon as I'm alone, the tears come. The distress of being abandoned. Recovering from dependence. Reluctantly. Learning to be autonomous again when I no longer want to be. Ambien and memories, burning like a delicious hot tea. Solitude and the burden of a secret too heavy to bear.

Time passes. One morning, in my office, there's a phone call from a man who says he's His friend.

I take the line. It's Philippe.

He's given him my telephone number, and permission to use it.